TH

JOURNAL

BELONGS TO

RATCHET

THIS JOURNAL BELONGS TO RATCHET

NANCY J. CAVANAUGH

SCHOLASTIC INC.

ISBN 978-0-545-65519-4

12 11 10 9 8 7 6 5 4 3 2 1   13 14 15 16 17 18/0

Printed in the U.S.A.   40

First Scholastic printing, November 2013

Cover design by Becky Terhune
Internal illustrations by Jillian Rahn

To Ron,
my best friend and biggest fan.

To Chaylee,
my gift straight from God.

And to my parents
for a lifetime of love and support.

HOMESCHOOL LANGUAGE ARTS JOURNAL

NAME: Ratchet

AGE: 11

Assignment:

Choose writing exercises from *Write From Your Life*, (*Homeschool Language Arts, Edition 5*).

Record your writing in a spiral notebook.

Include a variety of writing formats.

Writing Format—FREE VERSE POETRY: Poetry
that does not require regular rhythm or a rhyme
scheme.

If only getting a new life
Were as easy as getting
A new notebook.
But it's not.

Couldn't face another year
Writing on those
    Long,
    Yellow
    Legal
    Pads.
Dad found them at a garage sale.
They smelled like wet dog.

I bought this notebook

With clean white pages

Because this year I need

    White pages.

This year I need

    A cardboard cover

    In cool colors.

This year I need

    Something new to write on

    And to happen.

♥

Everything in my life is old and recycled.

* The kitchen table and chairs—Salvation Army.
* Living room furniture—AMVETS.
* TV—Motel 8's going out of business giveaway.

Even worse, I look like I belong in a museum of what not to wear with my Goodwill store clothes.

Dad's motto: "If the Good Lord wanted us to throw everything away, he would've put a Dumpster right outside the Garden of Eden."

I want to say, "Not likely, Dad", but I don't argue with him. Especially when he's talking about the Good Lord.

Even so, I wish we'd lose all this junk so we could start over. Because it's hard to look good in faded T-shirts that are too big. Jean shorts that are out of style. And my blond hair with no style at all thanks to coupons at Super Snips.

Today could be a day to start over. It's the first day of school for all the kids in the neighborhood. But not for me. I'm homeschooled. That means nothing new.

* No new book bag.
* No new clothes.
* No new shoes.
* No friends—new or old.

Just Dad and me and a bunch of smelly old textbooks from the library book sale. And a garage full of broken-down cars that need fixing.

So I sit at the chipped and dented kitchen table doing my assignments. Wishing I were in a real classroom. With real classmates. And a real teacher.

A teacher who says, "Good morning," and smiles.

A teacher who reads my assignments and writes "Great job!" and "Way to go!" on my papers with glitter pens and funky colored markers.

Dad just glances at my work without really reading it. I know he doesn't really read it because one time for a social studies paper I wrote, "Abraham Lincoln's nose is bigger than his hat," two hundred times. Dad put a check mark at the top of the paper and wrote, "Keep the engine running!"

It was proof that Dad did not really read my work and even more proof that Dad is really out there somewhere on some automotive planet all his own because who would write, "Keep the engine running!" on top of a paper about Abraham Lincoln?

As long as I do my homeschool work, Dad thinks he's being a great teacher.

Dad's out in the garage yelling, "Ratchet!"

I don't think he's ever called me by my real name, **RACHEL**. At least not since I can remember. Says I've always reminded him of a ratchet the way my help makes all his jobs easier.

I've been fixing cars with him since I was six.

Dad yells again, "I could use a hand out here!"

So I'll put down my pencil, even though I hate to because it's new. It's real wood. (Not the fake plastic kind.) Purple sparkles. A super sharp point. And a perfect eraser. But I'll put it down anyway and go out to the garage and hand Dad tools for the rest of the afternoon.

What would I _rather_ be doing? Getting off a _real_ school bus with some _real_ school friends after a _real_ day of school.

What _will_ I be doing? Maybe a brake job or a transmission flush or a fan belt replacement. Hopefully not another oil change. My hands are finally almost clean from the one we did last week.

None of the things an ordinary eleven-year-old girl _should_ be doing. But when your nickname is Ratchet, you're not an ordinary girl.

WRITING EXERCISE: Poetry

Between bites of

Macaroni and cheese,

Dad talks

About

Torque wrenches and trees,

About

Oil rings and the ozone layer,

About

Gaskets and global warming.

I scrape the bottom

Of my bowl

Wishing for something.

Hoping for something.

Waiting for something.

Something I worry will never come.

I look at Dad's

Crazy, tired eyes

And wish

I didn't wish

for so much.

Because I know Dad

Tries real hard.

WRITING EXERCISE: Write a descriptive essay about something that is important to you.

Writing Format—DESCRIPTIVE ESSAY: A factual piece of writing in which you give a clear, detailed picture of a person, place, thing, or event.

I have a silver chain with a blue stone on it. It's "my most important thing." Not because it's expensive. (I don't even know how much it cost.) Not because I love jewelry. (I don't even wear jewelry. It clashes with my out-of-style clothes. Besides, safety rule number two, right after "Always wear safety glasses when working on cars" is "No jewelry in the shop.")

The necklace is important because it was my mom's. And my mom is dead. This is the only thing I have of hers. She died when I was five. So I don't remember much about her. But when I hold the blue stone I remember her more. Like the feel of her hair. The smell of her neck. Her smile.

I have one photo of her. She's sitting on a rock at the beach. She's wearing a blue-checkered sundress. And the blue stone is hanging around her neck. The dark blue water and lighter blue sky are behind her. I wonder if this is why my favorite color is blue.

I touch the stone to my cheek and pretend I'm resting my head on my mom's arm. The necklace is "my most important thing" because it makes me remember things I never want to forget.

If I had more things like the silver chain with the blue stone that were Mom's, I bet I could remember more about her. I bet if I could remember more about her, I could be more like her. I bet if I could be more like her, I could somehow make things change.

WRITING EXERCISE: Choose a proverb and rewrite it to make it a truth about your own life.

Writing Format—PROVERB: A simple, yet popularly known and repeated saying, based on a common sense–type truth.

UNKNOWN PROVERB:

"Like mother, like daughter."

RATCHET'S PROVERB:

"finding out about Mom, means finding out about me."

WRITING EXERCISE: Write a problem/solution essay.

Writing Format—TWO-PART ESSAY: An essay requiring two different types of thinking about a subject.

My problem is: my life is not normal.

People say there's a solution to every problem. I'm not so sure.

One solution is for me to stop working on cars. But Dad would never get all the cars fixed on time without my help. And we wouldn't have any money.

Another solution is for me to go to school, but I'd have a better chance of becoming Miss America than that ever happening. Dad says, "The Good Lord gave me the good sense to know you're better off learning from me than some half-witted college graduate who doesn't know a gol' darn thing about the real world."

The Good Lord has given me the good sense to know I'll never see the inside of a school, but lately, I've been thinking, maybe Dad would agree to a class at the rec center. That might give me a chance at making a friend, and that would be a huge step toward normal.

My last solution is to find out more about Mom so that I can finally become who I'm really supposed to be.

WRITING EXERCISE: Poetry

Moms are the ones

Who make sure of a lot of things.

Like that their kids

Wear nice clothes,

Comb their hair,

Brush their teeth.

And Moms teach their kids

How to fold laundry

So their clothes aren't wrinkled,

How to make scrambled eggs

Without turning them brown,

How to make a girl feel like a girl.

How can a girl feel like a girl

Without a mom to make her

feel that way?

WRITING EXERCISE: Write a proposal for an upcoming project.

Writing Format—PROPOSAL: A specific, organized plan for solving a problem or doing a project.

SUBJECT: Ratchet

PROJECT DESCRIPTION: Turn my old, recycled, freakish, friendless, homeschooled, motherless life into something new.

PROJECT GOALS:

1. Make a friend.
   * Use magazine makeover tips to improve my look.
   * Sign up for "Get Charmed" class at the rec center.
   * Cross my fingers and hope to make a friend.
2. Be more like Mom.
   * Ask Dad questions about Mom.
   * Search for things that are Mom's to help me remember her.

* find things I might have in common with Mom.

<u>OUTCOME</u>: To be a girl who fits in—hopefully one with a friend.

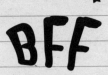

WRITING EXERCISE: Define a vocabulary word with a situational example.

Writing Format—Situational: A short scene written as an example of something

Vocabulary Word—Vague: not clear or not definite

"Dad, you know how you always say people should get involved in their communities?"

"Yeah," Dad said as he hunched over the open hood of an SUV.

"Well, there's this class at the rec center that I think might help me get involved."

"Oh, yeah?"

I didn't tell him the class was called "Get Charmed" and that the only community I'd <u>hopefully</u> be getting involved in would be a bunch of girls learning about manners and makeovers. I knew that wasn't really the community Dad was talking about.

"Yeah, it sounds interesting," I said.

Thankfully, Dad was having a hard time with the gasket he was trying to replace, so he didn't ask for any details.

"I guess it's all right," he said, without even looking up.

"It costs twenty dollars," I said, holding my breath.

"You can take money out of the coffee can in the kitchen."

"Thanks, Dad," I said.   (yes!)

"Now, c'mere and help me stretch this so I can get this doggone thing on."

While I helped Dad, I thought about how the rubber gasket wasn't the only thing I was stretching.

WRITING EXERCISE: Poetry

Writing Format—LIST POETRY: A form of poetry that lists words or phrases.

THINGS I'LL LEARN IN THE "GET CHARMED" CLASS

Latest fashion trends,

Helpful skin care,

Plus cool and funky hair tips,

And

Important social manners;

But

I'm hoping for what's not listed

In the rec center brochure.

A chance

To make

A friend.

WRITING EXERCISE: Use poetry to define attributes of a person close to you.

Thoughtfulness is

Dad buying sugar twist doughnuts

Every Saturday

Because I like them,

Even though he doesn't.

Kindness is

Dad pumping up

My bike tires for me,

Even though I could do it for myself.

Goodness is

Dad getting Disney movies

from the library

Even though he only watches documentaries.

Patience is

Dad letting me change my first flat tire

When I was only eight

All by myself,

Even though it took me an hour and a half.

Gentleness is

Dad staying up all night

And giving me ice chips

When I had strep throat,

Even though he was sick too.

WRITING EXERCISE: Write dialogue to show a character's personality.

Writing Format—DIALOGUE: Words spoken between characters.

"I think I found it!" I yelled as I felt a few drops on my cheek.

"Are you sure?" Dad asked.

He was standing over the engine of an old pickup truck we were working on, and I was underneath it. We were looking for an oil leak.

I wiped my cheek with a rag.

"Yeah, I'm sure. This has to be it," I said. I felt a few more drips. This time on my forehead. "Oh, wait! There must be another leak."

"A second leak?" Dad asked. "Are you sure?"

Just then brown liquid poured down on me, covering my safety glasses.

"Oh, man!" I yelled.

I couldn't figure out what was going on until I heard Dad

22

laughing, and then I smelled chocolate.

"Dad!" I yelled.

I wiggled out from under the truck and took off my safety glasses, which were dripping with chocolate sauce. I wiped my forehead with my rag.

"Got ya!" Dad said, laughing some more. "Want some?" he asked, holding up a plastic bottle of chocolate sauce.

"No thanks. I already had some."

Dad tipped his head back and squirted chocolate sauce into his mouth right out of the bottle.

"You can find the leak yourself," I said, trying to sound mad.

"I found the leak this morning before you got up," Dad explained. "Just thought I'd have a little fun. Sure you don't want some?" He squeezed another big squirt of sauce into his mouth, then grabbed my rag and flicked me in the arm with it.

I snatched the chocolate sauce from him and squirted some in my own mouth.

23

WRITING EXERCISE: Write a descriptive essay about something you have strong feelings about.

I HATE my dad's favorite T-shirt.

It says, "Is it me or is this place a festival of idiots?"

My dad wears this shirt to every city council meeting. Every meeting is shown on TV, and at every meeting, my dad stands up in this T-shirt and talks.

So, everyone, and I mean everyone, has seen my dad wearing this shirt. They all think he's crazy: because of the shirt, because his hair is fuzzy and too long and never combed, but mostly because of how he lectures the city council members.

He tells them they're ruining the planet by buying light bulbs that use too much electricity. He tells them they're scoundrels for letting their sprinklers water the parking lots. He tells them it's a farce how many trees they waste with all the paper they use. It's the same thing every time.

Dad always says, "If the Good Lord wanted us to be stupid, he wouldn't have put brains in our heads."

He really believes God's telling him to save the planet. He says it's his mission. I wonder if the Good Lord tells him anything about his T-shirt. I mean, I'm pretty sure the Good Lord doesn't appreciate Dad calling everyone idiots.

I wish my dad didn't wear this T-shirt. I wish he didn't go to city council meetings. Or get so disgusted that no one cares about the planet the way he does. I wish my dad were one of the guys at the city council meeting wearing a suit. I wish he sat quietly. I wish he never got up to talk.

This is why I HATE my dad's favorite T-shirt.

IS IT ME OR IS THIS PLACE A FESTIVAL OF IDIOTS?

WRITING EXERCISE: Write a descriptive essay about where you live.

This year we moved. Again. We move every year. Not to a new town. Just to a different neighborhood.

We've lived in so many houses I can't even remember them all. But I don't really have to. They're all pretty much the same. They're called "Handyman Specials."

This is how it works. Dad finds a house that's vacant. One that looks like it should be bulldozed down. (Some look like they'd fall down without a bulldozer.) He finds out who owns it. Tells them he'll fix up the house for nothing if we can live there for free.

It works every time. When the house looks good, Dad looks for another dump. And we start all over again.

★ Dad says, "The Good Lord blesses those who got the good sense to work with the hands he gave them."

★ If that were really true, Dad and I should've been blessed with a mansion by now. One with a butler and a maid.

☆

WRITING EXERCISE: Write a descriptive essay about where you live. (Part 2)

I don't like living in broken-down houses. And moving over and over again means I never make any friends. Especially because I don't go to school. Two houses ago, I <u>almost</u> made some friends. There were some other homeschooled kids who lived in the neighborhood. Their moms planned field trips for them. And the kids played at the park together sometimes. But by the time I found out about them, our house was fixed up. And it was time to move again.

The only kids I meet in the neighborhood are the ones who walk by our "Handyman Special" on the way to school or to their friends' houses. They look at me on the driveway helping Dad put on a new muffler or flush a radiator, and I know they're thinking I must be some sort of freak. To live in a house that's falling down. To work on cars in the driveway. To have a dad who looks like my dad. What else could they think?

So I normally don't even try to make friends. I pretend I'm invisible. And because of the way I look it usually works. Especially with girls. My old clothes, my greasy hands, my hair falling out of its ponytail. It's almost as if they think looking at me might make my freakishness rub off on them.

Boys are different. They still see me even when I'm trying to be invisible. But not in the way girls _want_ boys to see them. They see me as a target. A joke target. I'm a practice punching bag for their humor. The only person they love to make fun of more than me is Dad. He's an even easier target than I am.

This boy Hunter lives on my block. His best friend Evan lives one block over. And they've been brutal. They can't walk by without saying <u>something</u>.

"Look at the Grease Monkey and his little Monkey Girl."

I don't think they can help themselves.

Every neighborhood's the same. Different kids. Same trash talk. And in the world's largest dictionary, there isn't one single word that comes close to describing what it feels like.

That's why this year, I have to do something different. Something that will change what people notice about me.

WRITING EXERCISE: Choose a proverb and rewrite it to express two different personal truths.

UNKNOWN PROVERB:

"Laughter is the best medicine."

RATCHET'S PROVERB: (PART 1)

"Laughter is poison when you are the punch line."

RATCHET'S PROVERB: (PART 2)

"But laughter is a lifesaver when your dad's in the attic fixing the air vent and his leg comes through the ceiling of the garage when he misses the two-by-four he was supposed to step on, and the next thing you know his other leg comes through the ceiling too, but you know he's okay because he's laughing so hard his legs are swinging; and you laugh even harder than he does and spit out the water you were trying to swallow. And the whole thing is like a lifeboat on the

sinking *Titanic* because this kind of laughter takes
the venom out of the poisonous laughter, and you
know you're going to be okay."

>≫ HA HA HA! ≪<

WRITING EXERCISE: Write a review of a book, short story, or magazine article.

Writing Format—REVIEW: A way to express thoughts, feelings, and opinions about literature. Your response can be a journal entry, a poem, or an editorial letter.

Dear Editors of *Stylin' It,*

Are you kidding? Those skinny jeans? Those cropped sweaters? Those long scarves looped and tied in just the right way? And those hairstyles? Really?

When I look at your magazine, I can't help but wonder, who dresses like this? I wonder this until I look over to the Teen Junction section of the library and see four girls giggling as they all try to read from the same paperback book. They all look like they just stepped out of your magazine, and it makes me wonder what magazine it looks like I just stepped out of.

Yours truly,
Not a Cover Girl

WRITING EXERCISE: Write a process list.

Writing Format—PROCESS LIST: A list that shows steps or stages in a process.

1. Find a look in a magazine—one that might come close to being possible for me.
2. Go to Goodwill to buy clothes and accessories.
3. Put an outfit together.
4. Wear the outfit to the first "Get Charmed" class.
5. Introduce myself to the other girls in class.
6. Make my first real friend. (Hopefully.)

WRITING EXERCISE: Write a descriptive essay about the most important person in your life.

Dad would never win "father of the Year," but he's still my "most important person."

Dad is not normal. He's a crazy environmentalist, who says things like, "Turning a blind eye to science is unethical," and, "Our children should spit on our graves for the way we squander the goodness of the Good Lord." And my personal favorite, "It's a no-brainer that designing buildings with windows on the east and west is a colossal waste of energy. It should be a crime!"

Dad's mission to save the world means:

* He doesn't believe in buying anything new because he can fix everything.

* He doesn't believe in using up the environment because he says it's what the Good Lord gave us to take care of.

* And he really doesn't believe in worrying about what people think because when you're following orders from the Good Lord, why would you care what people think?

So most people think Dad's nuts.

But Dad's actually SMART. Not many people know the kind of stuff he does, like "miles above the Earth's surface, our stratosphere's ozone layer is thinning. This ozone hole is caused by chlorofluorocarbons which are created by man-made chemicals."

The problem is most people don't care about stuff like that, but Dad cares A LOT that "as our ozone layer gets thinner, more harmful UV radiation reaches the Earth's surface every day." This stuff is ALL he ever talks about, and it makes him sound like a real nut job.

I just wish he could at least look smart the way a normal dad looks smart, having a haircut like the dads you see on TV commercials and wearing the kind of clothes you see men wearing in the Sunday paper sale ads. But every day Dad looks the same—like a young Albert Einstein wearing a greasy T-shirt and ripped jeans.

Dad's friends call him "Raccoon Dog." (RD for short.)

"Raccoon" because he's so good with his hands. And "Dog" because anyone who can fix your car is man's best friend. I just call him "Dad." And no matter what he says, or what he does, or how un-normal he makes our life, he'll always be my "most important person."

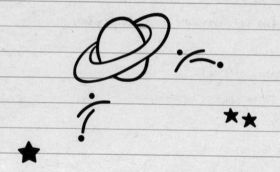

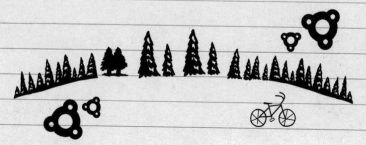

WRITING EXERCISE: Poetry

SUM POETRY #1

A trip to Goodwill is

= to

five racks of shirts

(Only two tops even cool enough to try on),

+

Six shelves of shorts

(Only three pairs in my size),

+

Three bins of shoes

(Only one pair even comes close).

WRITING EXERCISE: Poetry

SUM POETRY #2

One dark blue tank top
(With only a small snag in it),

One pair of tan shorts
(Which are only a little too baggy),

One light blue scarf
(Only frayed a little bit on one end),

One pair of shiny, silver flip-flops
(Only slightly ripped on one side)
Almost =

One cool look

from

Stylin' It.

WRITING EXERCISE: Write minutes to record a class or a meeting.

Writing Format—MINUTES: A summary of things discussed and decided on and also what action will be taken.

Blainesfield Recreation Center "Get Charmed" Class

PRESENT: Ms. Charlize (the teacher), Ratchet, and four girls who already look charmed.

3:50 I enter the classroom. No one else is there. I sit at the second table in the middle row.

3:54 Four girls enter, giggling and laughing. I recognize them from the library. They were the ones reading the paperback book together. They already look photo-shoot ready for a cover story in *Stylin' It.*

3:57 They finally notice me, but don't say hi. They squeeze closer together in a group, whisper a little too loud, "What's <u>she</u> doing here?" and then laugh.

3:58 Looking like one of the designers on a makeover show carrying her black leather portfolio in one hand, a dark-haired twenty-something click-clacks into the

room in superhigh heels, tight black jeans, and a black
sequined tank top with a sparkly black and green
scarf draped and looped in just the right way around
her neck. (It looks so much better than my slightly
frayed blue one, which is twisted around my neck
looking like someone's trying to strangle me.) "Hi,
girls! I'm Charlize!" she says, and smiles with teeth
that sparkle more than her scarf.

3:59 I stare at her—sort of mesmerized by the sparkles,
the sequins, and her smile.

4:00 She plops her portfolio on the front table and flips it
open. "How would you like to see my head shots?"

4:01 The *Stylin' It* cover girls rush the front table like
it's half-price day at the Dollar Store and gather
around Charlize and her photos.

4:02 "I love your hair in this one," cover girl #1 says.

4:03 "Look at those shoes!" says cover girl #2. "I want them!"

4:04 "These aren't even my best shots," Charlize explains
as she flips to another page in her portfolio with one
hand and flips her shoulder-length hair with the other.
"My agent keeps the really good ones," she says.

4:05 I'm still stuck in my seat at the second table in the
middle row. I can't see the photos from here, but I don't

want to. I've seen enough already. Seen enough to know that no matter how many racks and bins I go through at Goodwill, I will never be "charmed." This class isn't for people who want to "get charmed." It's for people who already "are charmed." And I'm not one of them.

4:10 I get up and head for the door, hoping to sneak out without being seen. But just my luck that Ms. Charlize picks this moment to notice me. "Sorry we haven't made room for you. Come on up and take a look." I feel everyone staring at me. And at that moment I wish I could be like Dad—not caring what anyone thinks. Not being afraid of what people say about me. Not worrying if I look like a fool in the Goodwill outfit I worked so hard to put together. But I do care. I came to this class because I care, and because I had hoped to make a friend, but I could tell that wasn't going to happen, so I just shrug and say, "I'm in the wrong room. This isn't the class I signed up for," which isn't even a lie.

4:11 I push open the double doors of the rec center and unlock my bike. I hop on and pedal away wondering where to go from here.

WRITING EXERCISE: Write a short monologue.

Writing Format—MONOLOGUE: A short entertaining piece that could be used as an expository reading.

NO STYLE REQUIRED

I get back to my room and look at myself in the mirror. I could see why they'd been staring. What had I been thinking? I looked like a little kid playing dress-up with that scarf draped around my neck. And the makeup I had put on made me look more like a clown than a supermodel. I had followed the step-by-step instructions in the copy of *Stylin' It* that I'd checked out from the library.

* Begin with Bayberry Blush and add Daylight Dusting Powder.
* Continue with Keep-Yourself-Covered Concealer.
* Add Elegant Eyeliner, Sure Shades Eye Shadow, and Midnight Moonlight Mascara.
* Paint on Periwinkle Nail Polish and spritz your neck and wrist with Seaside Sunshine Perfume.

* Accessorize your outfit with a scarf, belt, or
hat and step out in style.

I had followed the instructions carefully, but instead of
"stepping" out in style, I had just tripped. Actually, who was I
kidding? I had just fallen flat on my face.

I pick up the magazine, and even though I feel like
throwing it across the room like a frisbee, I open it.
Maybe there is some advice for a style misstep, but I find
something better. An article titled "Create Your Own
Style." So I unwrap the scarf. (It never really was me.)
I change into a white, cotton tank top. (Well, a tank top
that used to be white.) Then I pull on a light blue, short-
sleeved, button-down shirt and leave it unbuttoned. I kick
off the shiny, silver flip-flops, and I slip my bare feet into
my worn-out Keds.

I look at myself in the mirror again and wonder if anyone
would ever call an outfit like mine a "style." The thing is: it
doesn't really matter because any minute, my dad will be yelling
from the garage, "Ratchet! C'mere and hold this exhaust while I
put a clamp on it, would ya?" And even though my plan for this
afternoon had been to "get charmed," I'm thankful that Dad
needs my help and that no style will be required.

WRITING EXERCISE: Write a descriptive essay about a person you dislike.

Edward J. Johnson. AKA Eddie J. or Pretty Boy Eddie. He walks around town acting like he owns the place, and actually, he kind of does because he's so rich. He owns one restaurant, one gas station, three grocery stores, and one hardware store.

If this town were a kingdom, he'd be the king. If it were a country, he'd be the president. If it were the world, he'd think he was God. But it's only Blainesfield, so he's just a big shot. Dad says thankfully enough people still use the common sense the Good Lord gave them, so he's hasn't been elected mayor, not yet anyway, but he might as well be the mayor because skinny, squirrely Benson Prindle who really <u>did</u> get elected mayor, doesn't make a move without Eddie J.'s approval.

But these are not the reasons I dislike Eddie Johnson. I don't like him because of what he says to Dad.

"Why thank you for enlightening us with your highly scientific and most definitely accurate opinion about everything, Mr. Vance. We will take it all into careful consideration."

He says it as if he's talking to a stupid kid with crazy ideas, and he says it as if not one word of what Dad says is worth listening to, let alone worth "careful consideration." He's sarcastic and snotty. And he says the same thing to Dad every time Dad speaks at the city council meetings because Eddie J., of course, is the city council spokesman. That's why I dislike Edward J. Johnson.

WRITING EXERCISE: Write a narrative essay about your most embarrassing moment.

Writing Format—NARRATIVE ESSAY: A factual piece of writing in which you express your ideas by telling a story.

ONE OF MY MOST EMBARRASSING MOMENTS

Dad makes me read the newspaper every day for social studies. So this morning I went outside to get the paper from the driveway, and when I did, Hunter and Evan came up the street on their bikes. When they saw me, Evan said really loud, "Hey, Hunter, I wonder if Ratchet's dad can use his tools to break out of the slammer. I bet he's not so handy in handcuffs."

I didn't know what he was talking about until I picked up the newspaper and unrolled it. The blood drained from my head to my toes. I lost all feeling in my arms. Why? Because there on the front page I stared at a huge photo of my "most important person" in handcuffs. He was wearing another one of the T-shirts I hate.

This one says, "If idiots were trees, this place would be an orchard."

Now, on top of my dad being the most un-normal dad in the world, he's a convict too.

Yesterday I thought Dad was out at the junkyard looking for parts.

"Why buy a new starter, when you might be able to find an old one?"

How about because it's easier, Dad?

But Dad hadn't really been out hunting for a starter. No wonder he'd gotten home so late. At breakfast he'd told me some story about running into some old friends and stopping for dinner. (Unless he's friends with the Chase County Police Department, and they serve dinner down at the station in a holding cell, Dad had lied to me.) It wasn't the first time.

He said stretching the truth was sometimes necessary. To save the environment. Or to protect someone you love. (I wonder what the Good Lord thinks of Dad's little lying theory?)

The headline to the story about Dad read, "TRACTORS STOP FOR DEVELOPERS OF MOSS TREE PARK." The caption under Dad's photo said, "Environmental activist steals keys to construction vehicles in hopes of delaying development of Moss Tree Park."

In the article Dad says, "These morons think the only thing green is money. They're going down!"

I wonder why it's so hard for Dad to just keep his mouth shut.

Dad told reporters he'd found out that the guy who originally owned Moss Tree Park was Herman Moss. When Mr. Moss died and left the park land to the county, he supposedly had one condition—the land could never be developed.

Dad said he'd read about it in an old newspaper article he found at the library, but for all I know, the Good Lord told him about it in a dream.

Of course, no one can find the paperwork to prove what Dad says is true, but Dad told the newspaper he plans to somehow find it.

Mayor Prindle said, "It's too bad Mr. Vance can't channel all that passion he feels toward parks into something that will really benefit this town: and that's progress. I like parks as much as the next guy, but money doesn't grow on trees, Mr. Vance, and our town stands to gain a lot of revenue from this new strip mall."

I knew this was something Eddie J. had told him to say. Dad always said Mayor Prindle never spoke to reporters without talking to Pretty Boy Eddie first. He was good at knowing what to say when the cameras were rolling, but when they weren't, Pretty Boy and the mayor were much meaner.

Dad told me the mayor once called him, right to his face, "a raving lunatic with a warped view of reality." I guess Dad sort of deserved it with all the things he said at the meetings. He had called the city council members much worse things, but at least Dad wasn't two-faced. Pretty Boy Eddie always acted like such a nice guy in public, but the minute he wasn't on record, he turned into pretty much a jerk. Dad and Eddie J. had been at war with each other for years about everything, and Moss Tree Park was just one more battle.

I'm sure Dad had stolen the tractor keys, hoping his stunt would give him more time to do some investigating, and he was right. The article ended with, "No doubt the mayor and the city council should do some of their own investigating before moving forward with the Moss Tree Park project."

Dad loved fighting for places like Moss Tree Park, and he never gave up. Especially when it had to do with the environment. And if it wasn't <u>this</u> park or <u>these</u> trees, it would be something else.

That's why I know this is only ONE of my most embarrassing moments.

WRITING EXERCISE: Write a letter of complaint.

Writing Format—LETTER OF COMPLAINT: A type of business letter that states a problem.

Dear God,

Dad's supposedly doing work for you, and usually that ends up being only slightly annoying and somewhat embarrassing, but now I'm getting caught in the middle. Dad's arrest earned him one hundred hours of community service, but it's turning into _my_ punishment.

They've assigned Dad a class at the rec center. Every year there's a go-cart contest in Moss Tree Park. So the rec center has a "Build Your Own Go-Cart" class. They need a new teacher since they got rid of the last guy because he didn't know a flathead from a Phillips. They thought Dad would be perfect for the job, and Dad thinks I'll be perfect for the job of his assistant.

What this all means is that I'll be helping Dad with the go-cart class——which Hunter and Evan will be taking, <u>and</u> the

class meets right across the hall from the "Get Charmed"
class THE SAME DAY AND TIME!

It's bad enough I'm not "getting charmed," and now this.

I would appreciate any attention you could give this matter.

Sincerely,

Ratchet

WRITING EXERCISE: Respond personally to a famous quote.

PABLO PICASSO:

"When I was a child, my mother said to me, 'If you become a soldier, you'll be a general. If you become a monk, you'll end up as pope. Instead I became a painter, and I wound up Picasso.'"

RATCHET:

I don't know what my mom said I could be, so how will I know what I am supposed to become?

WRITING EXERCISE: Poetry

Writing Format—CONCRETE POETRY: A form of poetry in which the shape or design helps express the meaning or feeling of the poem.

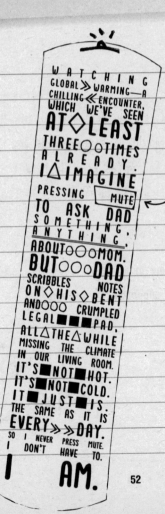

WATCHING
GLOBAL ≫ WARMING—A
CHILLING ≪ ENCOUNTER,
WHICH WE'VE SEEN
AT ◇ LEAST
THREE ○ ○ TIMES
ALREADY.
I △ IMAGINE
PRESSING │ MUTE │
TO ASK DAD
SOMETHING,
ANYTHING,
ABOUT ○ ○ ○ MOM.
BUT ○ ○ ○ DAD
SCRIBBLES NOTES
ON ◇ HIS ◇ BENT
AND ○ ○ ○ CRUMPLED
LEGAL ■ ■ ■ PAD.
ALL △ THE △ WHILE
MISSING THE CLIMATE
IN OUR LIVING ROOM.
IT'S ■ NOT ■ HOT.
IT'S ■ NOT ■ COLD.
IT ■ JUST ■ IS.
THE SAME AS IT IS
EVERY ≫ ≫ DAY.
SO I NEVER PRESS MUTE.
I DON'T HAVE TO.

I AM.

52

WRITING EXERCISE: Write a progress report.

Writing Format—PROGRESS REPORT: A report documenting progress made in regard to accomplishing a proposed goal.

Report on Progress of Proposal Goal #2—Be More Like Mom

Places I've Searched for Clues about Mom:

- Kitchen junk drawer
- Living room TV stand
- Dad's nightstand
- Linen closet storage bin
- Office desk drawer

Things I've found:

WRITING EXERCISE: Write questions to interview an expert about a specific topic.

Writing Format—INTERVIEW: Find an expert on your subject. Formulate important questions and record the expert's responses.

The only expert on Mom I know is Dad, so I imagine the interview questions I'd like to ask him.

1. What did you like best about Mom?
2. What did she like best about you?
3. What did Mom like best about <u>me</u>? (That's the question I really want to ask.)
4. What was her favorite color? Her favorite food? Her favorite TV show?

But when Dad and I are in the garage, working on grinding down some rotors, those questions seem as out of place as I was in my Goodwill outfit at the "Get Charmed" class. So I ask a question that I'd never thought of before, but one that seems to fit the situation better. "Hey, Dad, did Mom like cars?"

"What?" he asks, sounding confused, as he slides the caliper over the rotor.

"Mom. Did she like cars as much as you do? Did she ever help work on them like I do?"

"Not really" is all he says; and the way he says it, I know the interview is over before it has even begun.

WRITING EXERCISE: Updated Progress Report

Another day

I search again

for something of Mom's.

In cupboards

In closets

In dressers

And

Even bathroom drawers

But

find

Nothing.

Then I see

An old

Cardboard box

full of

Cotton balls

And Q-tips

Way in the back

Under the sink

In the second bathroom—

The one Dad's still fixing.

And when I see it

I remember

The box.

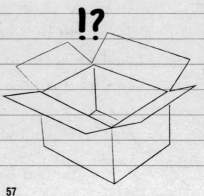

WRITING EXERCISE: Write a free verse poem about an object in your house.

THE MYSTERY BOX

There's a box.

It's cardboard.

It's taped shut.

And it hasn't been opened

For a long time.

You can tell

Because the tape

And the cardboard

Are melted together.

The box goes with us

To each "Handyman Special" we move into.

Sometimes Dad puts the box in his closet.

Sometimes he puts it in the laundry room

On a shelf.

Sometimes he puts it in a kitchen cupboard.

I wonder where

Dad's put it

<u>This</u> time.

In <u>this</u> house,

Because I haven't seen it lately

And I haven't found it,

Yet.

Maybe I can't find

Anything of Mom's

Because it's all

Inside

The box.

(I wonder what Dad would say if he read this.)

<u>THE OTHER BOX</u>

There is another box.

Not taped shut

Not up on the shelf

Not hiding in the closet

But here

With me

Every day

Usually hiding inside

A T-shirt

I hate.

We

Live together,

Eat together,

Work together

My dad and I.

So why don't I know what's inside?

THE THIRD BOX

My heart

Is the third box

Held together by hope

For something.

I don't even know what.

The hope keeps the box

Together.

And keeps everything inside.

So I hold on tightly

To the hope,

Afraid

To let go

Because

No one knows what's inside.

Not Mom.

Not Dad.

Not even me.

?

WRITING EXERCISE: Write an observation report about something you did this week.

Writing Format—OBSERVATION REPORT: A report that includes vivid details that appeal to all the senses.

At the Rec center, I walked down the hall. Thankfully, without being noticed by the cover girls. They were already crowded around Charlize, practically sitting on top of her. It looked like she had every kind of makeup ever made spread out on the front table. Eye shadow, blush, lip gloss, mascara, and I could smell perfume all the way out in the hall.

I turned and went into the room Dad had been assigned. Food wrappers and empty soda cans all over the floor. Desks pushed every which way. The air was a mixture of peanut butter and sweat with a faint smell of lemon floor cleaner. (Hard to believe you could still smell the floor cleaner because it looked like the floor in our garage, which has never been washed.) In the middle of the room were eight boys. All talking too loud.

Dad wasn't there yet. He was finishing up a brake job at

home. He sent me over on my bike to keep order until he got there. I wondered if he realized I was the same age as the kids in the class. What made him think I could keep order?

No one noticed me when I walked in. I picked up a few candy wrappers from the floor. Straightened out a few desks. (It did about as much good as throwing a cup of water on an overheating engine.)

Then Evan said, "Hey, look, everyone. It's Professor Ratchet!"

The kids laughed in a way that proved Evan was the "cool" kid everyone looked up to.

I ignored him. Maybe my invisible routine would work. I pushed a few more desks to make another row. That's when I smelled something like burned toast. Evan yelled, "FIRE!" And at the same time, the fire alarm went off. We all ran out of the room and down the hall with the screaming cover girls following us.

Out in the parking lot, an old lady waved her arms. "It's all right. False alarm. Little mishap in creative cooking. No big deal."

That's when Dad came squealing around the corner in his 1981 diesel Rabbit. (Real rabbits are quiet, cute, and cuddly; but there's nothing quiet, cute, or cuddly about Dad's piece of junk car.) The squealing noise came from the loose fan belt he never bothered to fix. He was always too busy fixing other people's cars to fix his own.

If it weren't for the smell of the fire, we would've <u>smelled</u> Dad coming before we heard him. To keep the environment cleaner, Dad had converted his car to run on vegetable oil. <u>Recycled</u> vegetable oil, of course. Which meant the oil came from fast-food restaurants. They threw out barrels of the stuff every day. Dad always picked up oil from King of Wings so he spread the tasty aroma of fried chicken wings wherever he went.

Dad waved at me through his open window as he pulled into the parking lot. Then the rec center director, who looked a little like Cruella de Vil, realized Dad hadn't been in his classroom when the fire alarm went off. She went CRAZY. As crazy as Dad did at the city council meetings.

"Mr. Vance! Where have you been?! You mean to tell me that you were not supervising your students when the fire alarm went off?"

Dad's car door groaned as he got out. The door barely opened and closed anymore. The car really belonged at the junkyard instead of on the road.

"Sorry. I was running a little late," Dad said as he got out. "Won't happen again."

Dad slammed the door. I cringed, hoping the whole car wouldn't fall apart. Dad's hair looked like it had been <u>fried</u> in vegetable oil. He had a huge oil stain on his shirt. Black wheel-bearing grease smeared into his knees. And his hands looked like they hadn't been clean in years.

The boys in the class looked at Dad and took Evan's lead—they all burst out laughing. The cover girls joined in. I could tell from the way they giggled that they thought Dad was a huge joke, and I could tell by the way they fluttered their eyelashes and looked over their shoulders as they huddled closer together that they wanted the boys to stop noticing Dad and start noticing them.

"Mr. Vance," Cruella went on, waving her finger in Dad's face (she even had long Cruella de Vil fingernails), "this whole arrangement of you teaching goes against my better judgment. You'll need to work a lot harder to prove me wrong."

"Yes, ma'am."

Dad knew he couldn't mess this up. It was community service or jail time.

Soon we got the "all clear" from the fire department who'd showed up a couple of minutes after Dad.

"C'mon, future mechanics of the world," Dad said, waving his arm toward the door. "Let's go build some go-carts."

Evan raised his eyebrows to the group. Then circled his finger by his head and mouthed the word crazy.

He'd read my mind. This was only the beginning.

CRAZY

WRITING EXERCISE: Poetry

Which one of these things
Doesn't belong?
Mayor Prindle and Pretty Boy Eddie
Dressed in suits
Dumping a recycling bin
 full of shredded paper
Into a dumpster hidden by trees
Behind the library.
Something tells me
More than one thing
Doesn't belong.

WRITING EXERCISE: Write a narrative essay about meeting a new person.

I was holding a flashlight for Dad. It felt like my arm was going to fall off. He was changing the fan belt on a minivan, which was a tricky job. And it was taking forever.

Sixties and seventies music blasted from the garage radio. I sort of hated to love Dad's music because I should've been listening to pop and rap like other kids my age. But I still sang along with every song.

That's why I didn't hear Hunter's mom come into the garage. I smelled lilacs. And then there she was. I jumped. The flashlight moved.

"Ratchet!" Dad yelled. "Hold still!"

Then he bumped his head on the hood of the car.

"Sorry!" Hunter's mom called out over the music. "I don't mean to bother you!"

I looked past her. Hunter sat in the front seat of the car. For some reason he looked like a little first-grader sitting there in the car by himself. I'd never seen him without Evan.

68

Dad pulled his head out from under the hood. "What's the problem?"

Dad always asked, "What's the problem?" People didn't come to our house for any other reason except problems. Car problems.

Hunter's mom looked worried. She explained she'd almost gotten into an accident that morning. She told Dad her car had died in the middle of traffic. She said she didn't know what to do.

People told Dad stuff like this all the time. But for some reason it sounded different when Hunter's Mom talked. I don't know if it was the lilac perfume. Or the way she used her hands to tell the story. Or just how pretty she looked in her sleeveless cotton shirt, matching capris, and flip-flops. Her hair was the same color as mine. And the same length. It was in a ponytail. But it looked <u>so good</u>. She was all put together like a mannequin in a store.

Dad told her we'd take a look at the car. But he had to finish the fan belt first. She and Hunter should leave the car there and walk home. Hunter's mom looked relieved.

Dad got back under the hood. I aimed the flashlight on the pulleys for the fan belt. I took a deep breath, smelling the last of the lilac perfume before it got swallowed up by the smell of grease and oil.

(I don't know <u>what</u> Dad would think if he read this.)

WRITING EXERCISE: Make a web about a person or place.

Writing Format—WEB: A graphic organizer that organizes important information into the shape of a web.

My web is about Hunter's mom. She picked up her car yesterday. The problem was only a bad spark plug wire. She paid Dad with a check. But she also brought us cookies. She still smelled like lilacs.

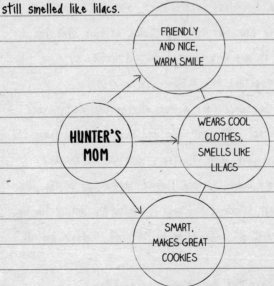

WRITING EXERCISE: Write a limerick.

Writing Format—LIMERICK: A silly five-line
poem with a specific rhyming pattern.

There was a young girl named Ratchet.
She had skill and no one could match it.
She wanted to be
More stylish and carefree,
But she couldn't give up her ratchet.

WRITING EXERCISE: Write a summary report of a class or club meeting.

DAD'S SPEECH AT THE LAST CITY COUNCIL MEETING

Dad stood at the microphone. He spat out words like he couldn't stand the thought of what he was saying. "You people are downright destroying the planet for the kids you pretend to care about."

Someone in the audience laughed. Dad shot him the "death look" (a look of disgust that would make the worst criminal crumble). The man slumped down in his seat.

Then Dad looked over the rims of his glasses like a crazy professor and went on. "Ocean acidification from too much carbon dioxide is already happening, and the warnings have been given by scientists about the risk of devastating our marine life and fisheries. And worse than that, higher levels of smog due to warmer temperatures potentially could increase respiratory illnesses."

Dad shook his head and went on. "And you, Mayor Prindle, catapault yourself into the twenty-first century with your statement in today's paper—'Global Warming: There just might be something to it.' It's about time you buffoon."

Dad grabbed his pile of crumpled notes from the podium, bumping the microphone and making a loud hollow sound before he walked back to his seat.

Pretty Boy Eddie said his usual comment to Dad in his usual smarmy way, and the next speaker in line looked like he wished he'd stayed home.

(Dad would be proud if he read this. Proud of himself.)

WRITING EXERCISE: Poetry

Dad is saving
The planet
for the Good Lord.
Sometimes
I wonder
If anyone
Is worried
About saving
Me.

!?

WRITING EXERCISE: Write about something that didn't turn out the way you expected.

I dreaded helping Dad with the go-cart class. For obvious reasons. The teasing. The jokes. The boys. The teasing. The jokes. The boys. But something surprised me.

It's not normal for me to know so much about engines. But it's more un-normal for the boys to know so little. Most of them didn't know a piston from a crankshaft. They didn't know an adjustable wrench from a combination wrench. And forget about knowing how to use the tools. They were clueless. It was kind of embarrassing.

So when it came time to build their engines, the jokes came to a screeching halt. They needed too much help. Dad couldn't help everyone at the same time; but when he was busy, I could help. So they all started being A LOT nicer to me. I didn't trust them at first. Thought maybe they were planning some big prank. But when I saw that most of them didn't even know which way to turn a screwdriver, I knew none of them were smart enough to be planning a prank AND building an engine.

They couldn't believe I knew exactly how to do everything.
I was living up to my nickname. Making everyone's job easier.

All day long, it was, "Hey, Ratchet, can you c'mere a
minute?"

"Hey, Ratchet, how do I get these oil rings on?"

"Hey, Ratchet, can you show me how to use this torque
wrench?"

Even without Charlize's tips for being charmed, I was
getting noticed.

WRITING EXERCISE: Write a multiparagraph answer.

Writing Format—MULTIPARAGRAPH ANSWER: Thoughts organized into more than one complete paragraph in order to answer an essay question.

WHAT DID DAD FIND OUT ABOUT MOSS TREE PARK FROM HERMAN MOSS'S NIECE?

Dad found out that Herman Moss has one relative still alive—a niece who lives in England. Dad thought she might know something about the park, so he found her number and called her.

She told Dad that every year on her birthday, she got a card from Uncle Herman with a photo of a tree that he planted in her name somewhere on one of his pieces of property. His card always said:

"Shade for man
And shelter for animals,
Planted in your name,
May you be the same for those around you,
Every year the same."

She had saved all the photos and cards and still had them in a box.

She knew that when her uncle died, he had donated all the land he owned to different counties, and all that land had been made into parks. But she didn't know anything specifically about Moss Tree Park.

Dad was hoping she would have some important family papers that would prove Mr. Moss didn't want the park developed, but she didn't. She said she was sorry and wished Dad good luck.

WRITING EXERCISE: Use a cycle diagram to illustrate a cycle of events.

Writing Format—CYCLE DIAGRAM: A diagram that shows the steps of a cycle in a visual way.

SUBJECT: MY LIFE

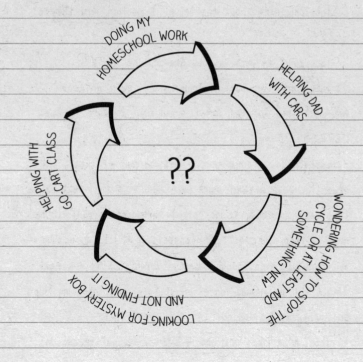

DOING MY HOMESCHOOL WORK

HELPING DAD WITH CARS

WONDERING HOW TO STOP THE CYCLE OR AT LEAST ADD SOMETHING NEW.

LOOKING FOR MYSTERY BOX AND NOT FINDING IT

HELPING WITH GO-CART CLASS

??

You would think kids who want to build go-carts would be grateful to someone who's trying to help them. But I never realized something _really_ important.

BOYS ARE JERKS!

They only care about one thing. Themselves. And they're JERKS!

They don't respect anyone. And they're JERKS.

They don't even care if someone else gets in trouble for what they do. And do you know why? Because they're JERKS!

Everything was going great. Well, maybe not great, but okay. The boys weren't being such wise guys anymore because they were too busy _trying_ to get their engines built. (Which none of them were getting much better at.) I was enjoying my popularity even though I knew it might not be for real. They'd still be making fun of me if they didn't need my help so much, but I tried not to think about that.

Then, as a joke, someone in Dad's class put grease on

all the doorknobs at the Rec Center. No one could open any doors anywhere in the whole building. Some little kid in the arts and crafts class peed his pants because he couldn't get the bathroom door open.

Cruella de Vil of course went ballistic and blamed Dad because his class is the only one that uses oil and grease. She said he should've controlled his class better. So now Dad's in trouble. Cruella's going to report him to Mr. Jenkins, the community service officer. They might even cancel the class.

If Dad has to do his community service hours picking up garbage instead of teaching this class, I'll die for sure. That wouldn't be <u>too</u> embarrassing, having Dad on the side of the road in one of those ugly orange vests. Ugh!

And all this is happening because boys are JERKS!

WRITING EXERCISE: Journal Writing. Choose from one of the six journal writing types.

Writing Format—LIFE EVENTS JOURNAL:
A record of daily events, experiences, and observations, as well as some personal reflection.

Today the phone rang while Dad and I were flushing the transmission on a Ford. I turned down the radio and answered it.

It was Community Service Officer Jenkins looking for Dad.

All I could think was, this was it! He was calling to ask Dad's size for the bright orange vest.

When Dad scooted out from under the minivan on the creeper he was lying on, I think he already knew who it was. He reached for the phone without even getting up.

I could tell from the look on his face, it wasn't good news.

So when he handed the phone back to me, I asked what Officer Jenkins said.

That's when Dad went into one of his usual rants. "What do you think he said? They found another teacher for the go-cart class, and now I'm gonna be working pollution pickup on the side of the road.

"If people didn't treat the Good Lord's green grass like it was the inside of a garbage can, there wouldn't even be any trash to pick up. I'm sure Pretty Boy Eddie's got something to do with this new 'community service assignment,' and as usual, he's got everyone eating out of the palm of his hand. Those crazies down at the sheriff's office have the backbone of a jellyfish. They're wasting more time worrying about punishing someone like me when I'm trying to educate the community about the ludicrous..."

Dad slid the creeper and himself back under the Ford and kept talking, but I couldn't hear him until he rolled out again and said, "You know what, Ratchet?"

I knew whatever he was going to say I had heard at least a dozen times before, but I still said, "What?"

"Those idiots would spend their time rearranging deck chairs on the *Titanic*. They don't even have the sense to use the brains the Good Lord gave them."

I was right. I had heard it all before. More than a dozen times. Probably more like a million.

"They want me to pick up garbage on the highway? I'll pick up garbage on the highway, but if they think that's going to stop me from fighting the crimes those fools at city hall commit every day when they allow developers to build schools and city buildings with windows facing the east and west, they're on a quick trip to crazy. How energy inefficient are they trying to be? And now disgracing a good man like Herman Moss to build another strip mall, just so some fools can sell more plastic garbage. They really make me sick," he added before he slid back under the car.

Then he slid back out again. "And you mark my words, Ratchet, you can be sure that crooked excuse for a man Eddie J. is planning to somehow line his pockets with green from this whole strip mall deal, and I'll be doggoned if I'm going to let him tear down the riches the Good Lord gave this town to make himself a wealthy man."

All this stuff matters to Dad, but the only thing that matters to me is that he's going to be wearing an orange vest and picking up trash on the side of the highway in broad daylight where everyone will be able to see him.

WRITING EXERCISE: Poetry

THE ONLY THING WORSE

> The only thing worse
>
> Than my life before,
>
> Is my life now.
>
> Because
>
> Garbage smells worse
>
> Than oil and grease.
>
> Orange vests look worse
>
> Than mechanic's clothes.
>
> And a community service criminal
>
> Is even more fun to tease
>
> Than a crazy mechanic.

WRITING EXERCISE: Poetry

THE ONLY THING WORSE #2

The only thing worse

Than Dad's crazy, embarrassing

Save-the-environment stunts

Is Dad just home from picking up trash.

Because he's

Dirty

Smelly

Sunburned

And I know he'd never admit it

But I can tell.

He's humiliated.

And even though

I hate being embarrassed,

Having Dad be embarrassed

Is even worse.

86

WRITING EXERCISE: Life Events Journal

I biked to the Gas Gulp Mini-Mart today for a frozen drink and ran into Hunter, Evan, and a few other boys from the go-cart class.

"So how's the jailbird doing?" Evan yelled when he saw me.

The other boys laughed. I wasn't surprised that outside of class I was back to being noticed for all the wrong reasons.

I ignored them and went inside to get my drink.

By the time I came out, the cover girls had shown up. They must've already been learning a lot at the rec center because they looked more like Charlize than the last time I'd seen them. And whatever she was teaching them was working because the boys were definitely noticing them.

When Evan saw me, he said, "We'll be sure to throw our candy wrappers on the ground so your dad doesn't run out of things to pick up while he's working the chain gang."

Their laughter made me wish I'd never been noticed by anyone for anything at all.

I pedaled my bike hard and fast toward home wishing...

Wishing...

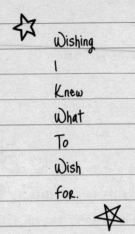

Wishing
I
Knew
What
To
Wish
for.

WRITING EXERCISE: Poetry

Dad always says
    If the Good Lord wanted us to do this...
      If the Good Lord wanted us to do that...
What I wonder is
Does the Good Lord
Care about us
As much as he cares about
    The trees
      And the grass
        And the decisions made
          At the city council meetings?
And if he does,
    Wouldn't he have made it harder
      for someone's feelings to get hurt?

WRITING EXERCISE: Life Events Journal

The next day I biked to Mama Mack's, the burger place in town, to get some dinner for Dad and me. The sky was getting dark, and I could smell rain, so I hurried. As bad luck would have it, when I got there, Hunter, Evan, and the group were outside. They were all crowded around one of their bikes. I hurried inside but not quick enough. I knew Hunter spotted me.

I ordered right away, paid, and headed back out to my bike with my food. Just as I put my bag into the milk crate on the back of my bike, there was a huge crack of thunder. The ground shook, and the restaurant windows rattled.

"Holy cow!" one of the boys said.

"Sorry, Evan, we're out of here!" another boy said, getting on his bike.

The sky got darker and the wind picked up, but the rain still didn't come. All the boys except Evan and Hunter rode away.

As I hopped on my bike, I realized that one of their bikes had a chain off the gear. Hunter and Evan were trying to put it back on with their fingers, but they were trying not to get their hands greasy. They were acting like the chain was a poisonous snake, and they were afraid to touch it. It looked like they had a better chance of getting struck by lightning than they had of getting that chain back on.

Another bolt of lightning and crack of thunder made us all jump. That's when I saw Hunter glance at me. I hopped off my bike and walked over.

I told them if they could find a stick, I could fix it.

"Yeah, right," Evan said.

Hunter looked around and grabbed a nearby stick on the ground under a bush and handed it to me. I put the stick inside the loop of the chain.

I told them to hold up the seat and get the rear wheel off the ground.

Evan did, and I pushed the pedal forward slowly, while I guided the chain back onto the gear with the stick. It clicked right into place.

Hunter smiled at me but didn't say anything.

Evan just said, "Hot dog! Let's go!" and hopped on his bike.

"Aren't you even going to say thanks?" Hunter asked.

"Oh, yeah, thanks," Evan said over his shoulder. "Surprised you didn't get your hands greasy. Oh, yeah, they already are greasy, never mind!" Evan yelled as he pedaled away.

Hunter didn't even turn around.

WRITING EXERCISE: Write step-by-step instructions for doing a common everyday task.

DIRECTIONS FOR REMOVING GREASE AND GRIME FROM HANDS AFTER WORKING IN THE GARAGE

1. Soak a rag in gasoline. Rub the rag over your hands, front and back. Caution: all your cuts and hangnails will hurt like crazy.
2. Take a palm full of Goop and rub front and back of hands, smoothing it all over.
3. Wash hands in laundry tub with Lava.
4. Repeat step three with Zest.
5. Wash hands again in kitchen sink with lemon-scented dish soap.

Note: If you follow these steps, your hands will technically be clean, but they won't look or feel like it. There will still be dirt and grime in most of the creases and crevices of your hands. They will smell like Goop, which smells like evergreen-scented car air freshener and oil mixed together. They will feel like sandpaper.

Most likely, and most importantly, a boy would not ever want to hold one of these hands.

WRITING EXERCISE: Write a short scene or story demonstrating first-person point of view.

Writing Format—FIRST-PERSON POINT OF VIEW: A story written from the main character's perspective.

I'm practically inside the huge cupboard under the sink in the laundry room looking for the hand lotion. I know it's in here in a big, ugly, green bottle. Dad said he saw it not too long ago. I'm thinking if my hands can't look good, maybe they can at least smell a little better than they do right now.

I'm wondering to myself: Where is that lotion? Why is there so much junk under here? And what is that weird smell?

Just when I'm ready to give up on having soft skin and sweet-smelling hands, I see something. The box. The one with the cardboard and tape melted together. The one Dad never opens. The one that I hope holds clues about Mom. And I feel like things seem softer and smell sweeter than they have in a long time.

I almost don't hear Dad yell from the garage, "Did you find it?"

His voice reminds me that my hands still smell bad and look even worse. But I'm hoping that what's inside the box will smooth out a lot more than rough skin.

"Not yet!" I yell back, answering my own question of when will I get to see what's inside the box.

As soon as Dad is gone again, my "not yet" will be now.

WRITING EXERCISE: Write a modern day fable. Include a moral at the end.

Writing Format—FABLE: A fictitious story meant to teach a moral lesson; characters are usually talking animals.

One day a raccoon named Ratchet went to the rec center where her father RD once taught a class. She went to pick up some tools her father had left there. She was surprised when she arrived at her father's old classroom to find all his raccoon students there. They were being taught by Evan's older brother, Steve.

Evan was the class troublemaker. He was always getting into trouble in the neighborhood knocking down garbage cans and sneaking into people's garages. His older brother, Steve, who went to raccoon junior college, was an even bigger troublemaker. He had been in so much trouble that once he had been caught in a trap and taken out to the country. He had somehow made his way back home by hiding in the back of a fruit delivery truck.

The students in RD's class were trying to put together

go-cart engines, but there was no way these go-carts were going anywhere. At least not unless someone helped the boys figure out how to turn their piles of engine parts into working engines. But their new teacher, Steve, was too busy talking and showing off to the cute college-age girl raccoon across the hall who was teaching younger girl raccoons how to brush and fluff their fur and wave their tails a certain way to impress the boy raccoons.

When the boys saw Ratchet, their faces lit up with excitement.

"Look, you guys," a boy raccoon named Hunter said. "Ratchet's here!"

Ratchet felt unusually glad to be noticed, but her gladness changed instantly when the troublemaker Evan said, "Aren't you supposed to be out on the highway somewhere holding a trash bag?"

Ratchet grabbed the torque wrench and spark plug gauge she came for and headed for the door.

"Wait!" the other raccoons cried after her. "Stay here and help us!"

"Let her go," Evan said. "She's probably got to go wash her dad's orange vest or something."

"No, we need her," someone said. "C'mon back, Ratchet!"

But Ratchet left, never looked back, and smiled all the way home.

THE MORAL: THERE'S NOTHING LIKE THE SATISFACTION OF BEING NEEDED.

WRITING EXERCISE: Write a concrete poem about a household item.

Writing Format—CONCRETE POEM: A poem that takes the shape of its subject.

RACHEL OR RATCHET

Am I just a person who knows

RACHEL/RATCHET/RATCHET/RACHEL?////

Which way to turn a screwdriver?

WRITING EXERCISE: Personal Journal

*Writing Format—*PERSONAL JOURNAL: A record of daily experiences with personal reflection on emotions and relationships with family and friends.

Today I asked Dad about the mystery box. I wasn't planning to ask him about it. I don't know why I did it.

Maybe it was because lately I'd been holding Mom's blue stone while I fell asleep at night wishing there was something else of Mom's I could hold on to. Or maybe it was because Dad hadn't been gone at all this week, and I'd never had the chance to be home alone so that I could drag that box out from under the sink and open it up. Or maybe it was just because I was dying to know what was in it.

Dad and I were working on a blue Chevy. Changing the fuel filter. And I just blurted it out.

"So, Dad, what's in that taped-up box under the sink in the laundry room?"

I knew by the look on his face I shouldn't have asked the question. But I couldn't take it back.

He stopped what he was doing. Put down his tools. Brushed off his pants.

"I gotta run for some parts." And he disappeared in the Vegetable Rabbit.

At first I felt like crying. Dad never ignored me when I asked a question.

But then I got mad. The box was in our house. It was probably Mom's. I should be allowed to know what's in it.

WRITING EXERCISE: Poetry

Writing Format—END RHYME: Write a poem using end rhyme (the rhyming of words at the ends of lines of poetry). Label the rhyming pattern.

I am hurt. I am <u>mad</u>.	**A**
At all the silence I get from <u>Dad</u>.	**A**
About the mystery box he's <u>hidden</u>	**B**
And all the memories he's <u>forbidden</u>.	**B**
Losing Mom is so <u>unfair</u>.	**C**
He doesn't even seem to <u>care</u>	**C**
That keeping her box away from <u>me</u>	**D**
Makes things worse than they have to <u>be</u>.	**D**

(I wished I had the guts to show this poem to Dad.)

WRITING EXERCISE: Life Events Journal

I went under the sink in the laundry room to get more rags for the garage, and the second I opened the cupboard, I knew something was wrong.

Bottles, cans, and jars of junk were scattered every which way. My heart pounded because my gut told me Dad had been in there, and it had been for one reason only. So when I crouched down and crawled partway into the cupboard, I wasn't surprised to see that the mystery box was gone.

I knew Dad had taken it, but I still turned everything upside down under there hoping by some miracle it would be hidden somewhere, but it wasn't.

Why would he move it? Did he think I'd try to open it? I should've opened it when I had the chance.

Now I'm REALLY MAD at Dad. (internal rhyme)

Operation Mystery Box starts today.

I'm going to find that box if it's the last thing I do.

And when I do, I'm not going to waste any time opening it.

WRITING EXERCISE: Poetry

Staticky talk radio buzzing,

Butter knife on toast scraping,

Newspaper pages rustling,

Cornflake spoon clinking,

And not much talking

Usually.

But lately,

The usual quiet

filling up the breakfast noise

feels quieter

Than usual,

feels fuller

Than usual,

And so it feels

Unusual.

I used to not talk

Because

I'm not a morning person.

Now I don't talk

On purpose

Because

Of Dad

And the box.

I looked up from the tire I was filling with air, and there they all were—the boys from the go-cart class—parking their bikes on the driveway. Thankfully, I didn't see Evan with them.

"Hey, Ratchet!" Jason said. "Is your dad here?"

I told them no.

They groaned, and Sean whispered to Jason, "Just ask <u>her</u>."

"<u>You</u> ask her," Jason whispered back.

But it was Hunter who asked, "Do you think your dad would teach us to build our go-carts here in your garage?"

I asked them what happened to Evan's brother.

"He's a doofus," Sean said.

★ "And he doesn't have a clue," Jason added.

I felt a spark somewhere inside me. It felt like hope.

★ "I'll ask him," I said.

WRITING EXERCISE: Write a short scene or story demonstrating third-person point of view.

Writing Format—THIRD-PERSON POINT OF VIEW: A story written as if you're telling what is happening to someone else.

Tension filled kitchen: the city council had just announced more bad news about the park. Ratchet's dad was scheduled to pick up trash in the morning. And Ratchet had been punishing her dad with silent anger for the last week. All this made it tough for Ratchet to ask her dad about teaching the go-cart class in the garage.

She thought sloppy joes would be the perfect supper to pave the way for her dad to say yes. But she was wrong.

"Ratchet, if you haven't noticed, I'm a little busy. There's a lot going on right now," her dad said.

She knew it hadn't been the right time to ask, but she was afraid to wait. She was afraid the boys might change their minds or find someone else to do the class.

But she wasn't just afraid. She was excited too! Excited for the chance to be noticed again in a good way. That's what made her keep asking, which is something she never did.

"C'mon, Dad," she begged. "They really need you. They can't build the go-carts without you."

What she didn't say was, "Dad, I really need you to do this for me because it's my chance for something different to happen."

"Ratchet!" her dad snapped.

His voice had turned city council stern.

"I've got twenty hours a week on the road picking up garbage, meetings every night this week with the mayor and his puppets, and cars parked up and down both sides of the driveway. What do you want me to do?"

Ratchet blinked in surprise at her dad's reaction. She wanted to say, "Pay attention. I. Want. You. To. Pay. Attention."

But she didn't say that because she knew her dad was paying attention, but to all the wrong things.

Her dad got up and said, "Thanks for supper, Ratchet," and kissed the top of her head before he walked back out to the garage.

Ratchet knew he felt bad. She knew he was stretched tighter than a fan belt on a pulley, but she was still mad. She was mad at him for saying no and mad at herself for not being able to tell him she needed him to save the class as much as he needed to save Moss Tree Park.

In the quiet kitchen she whispered, "Dad, I really need this," but no one was there to hear her.

WRITING EXERCISE: Write an opinion statement.

Writing Format—OPINION STATEMENT: A statement that expresses your opinion about an important subject. Create two or three supporting statements to back up your opinion.

Opinion: Teaching the go-cart class in our garage by myself is a good idea.

Supporting facts:

1. The boys need a teacher. (Proven fact)
2. I know how to build a go-cart. (Proven fact)
3. Dad won't mind if I help the boys build the go-carts as long as we don't get in his way. (Not so proven fact)

WRITING EXERCISE: Life Events Journal

Today all the boys came up the street pulling wagons full of their engine parts. Thankfully, Dad was out on garbage duty at the time.

They had never come back to see if Dad had agreed to let them have the class in our garage. I guess they thought if they just showed up, he couldn't say no.

"Is your dad gone again?" Jason asked, looking around.

"Yeah," I answered.

"Well, did you ask him?" Sean asked.

"He said it was okay," I answered quickly before I gave myself the chance to chicken out. "He told me to get you guys started without him."

"Cool," Sean said.

"Let's do it," Jason added.

So the boys sat down on the garage floor, and I

explained the four-stroke cycle using Jason's small engine to demonstrate it. When I finished, everyone started working on their engines, and they seemed to forget all about Dad coming back. Everyone that is, but me. I really didn't know what he would do if he came home and saw all the boys working in the garage. Thankfully, they left before he showed up in his orange vest, so I didn't have to find out.

WRITING EXERCISE: Life Events Journal

The next afternoon the boys came back, and this time Dad <u>was</u> home. I was helping him check the struts on someone's Oldsmobile when the wagons came squeaking up the driveway.

"Hi, Mr. Vance," they all said.

Dad looked at me.

I looked at my worn-out Keds.

Before Dad could even say anything, the boys were taking their engines out of the wagons and spreading them out in the garage.

"Ratchet, I think I get the four-stroke cycle now," Sean said, pulling a folded-up piece of notebook paper out of his pocket. "I drew a diagram of it last night, so I'd remember how you explained it."

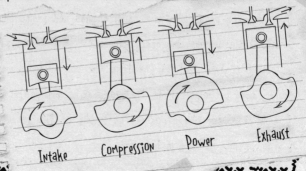

Intake   Compression   Power   Exhaust

I didn't say anything, but I didn't have to. Dad did.

"I don't know what you kids are doing here, but I've got work to do," Dad said. He didn't sound mean about it, just matter-of-fact.

The boys stood frozen, hovering over their engines not knowing what to do. I felt them staring at me, but I couldn't look up.

"What if Ratchet helps us?" Hunter asked.

That's when I did look up, and I saw Hunter looking right at me.

"That'd be hard for her to do when she's already helping me. Ratchet's my right-hand man out here in the garage."

That's when I felt my silent anger at Dad turning into something I'd never felt before.

"Go on, boys," Dad said. "Take your engines back up to the rec center. I hear they've got another teacher for y'all over there."

As the boys put their small engines and engine parts back into their wagons, my heart pounded in my ears. I still hadn't looked at Dad. But by the time the boys' wagons were so far away I couldn't hear them squeaking anymore, I stared right at Dad, who stood in the middle of the garage adjusting the wrench he held in his hands.

I pulled off my navy blue lab coat, which I wore now in hopes of keeping my new Goodwill clothes a little cleaner, and threw it on the floor.

"You can fix the struts yourself," I said.

I said it so quietly I wasn't sure Dad heard me, but I know he heard me when I slammed the door as I went inside. He had to—the kitchen windows rattled, and I heard the wrench Dad had been holding in his hands clatter to the floor.

WRITING EXERCISE: Write a scene for a play that shows a character's attitude.

Writing Format—SCENE: A section of dialogue from a play.

A normal day in the garage. Oldies music playing in the background.

DAD: Let's jack this car up and check the front brakes.

RATCHET: (Remains silent)

Ratchet adjusts the jack and cranks it four times. Chut, chut, chut, chut. And the car is off the ground. Dad puts the safety stands under the car.

DAD: Hand me the air gun.

RATCHET: (Remains silent)

Ratchet hands Dad the air gun, and Dad uses it to remove the tire.

DAD: I can't get a good look. Grab the light and plug it in.

Ratchet takes the light from the workbench, hands it to Dad, and then plugs it into the extension cord. Dad turns on the light and looks inside the caliper.

DAD: Yeah, they're worn. Put this one on the list for tomorrow.

RATCHET: (Remains silent)

Ratchet grabs the clipboard, and while she writes on it, she wonders if Dad even notices that she hasn't said one word.

WRITING EXERCISE: Poetry

Being noticed

for something

You're good at

feels almost

As good

As the cover girls look.

Actually,

I think it feels

Even better

Because

The cover girls

All look alike

And there are lots of them,

But there's only one

Me.

So I'll

Tell Dad

I'm still going

To "Get Charmed,"

But instead

Go down to

Hunter's house

And in the garage

Charm the boys

Into building go-carts.

And who knows?

By the time I'm finished,

I may be on my way to

Creating my own style.

WRITING EXERCISE: Life Events Journal

The next afternoon, while Dad was out picking up garbage, I walked down to Hunter's house. He was out in his garage. Thankfully by himself. (Actually it would have been nice if his mom had been there. I always liked to see what she was wearing.)

"How about I help you guys with your go-carts down here—in your garage," I said from the end of the driveway. I was afraid if I got too close, Hunter might be able to hear my heart pounding. I didn't know if I was more nervous about talking to Hunter or about doing something behind Dad's back.

Hunter looked up and walked toward me. "Really, you would? But what about your dad?"

"I'll figure it out."

I tried to sound cool about it, but I wondered if my voice gave away the fact that hearing Hunter be so excited about me agreeing to do this was almost more than I could take.

"All right, how about tomorrow?"

"Okay, see you," I said, and as I walked home, I thought about how surprised I was that it had been so easy.

Now all I had to worry about was Dad. 120 ☹ ?

WRITING EXERCISE: Life Events Journal

When we met in Hunter's garage the next day, the boys kept thanking me over and over again.

"Ratchet, if it weren't for you, we would've had to crawl back to Evan's brother," Sean said.

"Yeah," Jason added. "And none of us wanted to do that."

"Evan told us we were crazy when he found out you were helping us," Sean said. "But we'll all be surprised if Evan and his brother can even build a go-cart that works. His brother is so full of it."

I felt full of it too, but I didn't let it show.

Later while they were working on their engines, Sean said, "Hey, Hunter, stop hogging Ratchet. She's here to help all of us!"

"Maybe he's only pretending to need her help so much," Jason said. Then Jason raised his eyebrows up and down.

And the rest of the boys said, "Ooooh!"

Hunter's face turned red, and he didn't ask for any more help after that. I wondered if he was embarrassed about needing so much help or about the boys thinking maybe he liked me.

WRITING EXERCISE: Practice writing similes.

Writing Format—SIMILE: Comparisons using "like" or "as."

Like a car that ran out of gas, like a tire without air, like a compressor without any pressure, like a radio without any batteries, like I had been punched in the stomach, like I had been hit over the head, that's how I felt when I looked in the recycle bin after breakfast.

On top of all the other junk was the cardboard from a flattened-out box. Not just any cardboard from any box, but the cardboard from <u>The Box</u>. The one from the laundry room cupboard. The mystery box. It wasn't a box anymore. It was as flat as a pancake.

I recognized the cardboard because it was discolored and the tape was melted into it from being taped shut for so long.

I dug underneath it to see if Dad had dumped out what was inside the box too, but all I found were flattened cereal boxes and old newspapers. Where was the stuff from the box? Had he dumped it somewhere else?

Dad's crazy work for the Good Lord and him not agreeing to teach the go-cart class were one thing, but this was something else. Something that would change things between Dad and me forever.

As sure as an engine will burn up without oil, that's how sure I was that if Dad destroyed what was in the box, I would never, _ever_ forgive him.

WRITING EXERCISE: Poetry

My silent anger

Turns into

Shutting

Cupboards,

Doors,

And

Drawers

A little too hard,

But that isn't

The only thing

Slamming shut.

The door to

My

Heart

And

My

Soul

Slams

So

Hard

It comes off

The hinges.

Today I stood on the driveway hosing off some old hubcaps Dad found at the junkyard yesterday. I looked up and saw Hunter coming down the street on his bike. I wondered if he still felt weird about the other boys teasing him about me.

He stopped at the bottom of the driveway where I stood in a puddle of muddy water.

"Hey," he said.

"Hi."

Neither one of us said anything after that.

It was always easy to think of things to say when I was helping the boys with their go-carts. But now, what was there to talk about?

Finally Hunter started talking.

He told me about how he kept asking his dad if the two of them could rebuild an old car together, like the ones at those car shows up at Mama Mack's on Friday nights. Maybe a '57 Chevy—bright red or that cool turquoise blue.

I wondered why he was telling me all this?

Then he asked if my dad had ever rebuilt an old car like that.

And when I told him about the '55 Thunderbird, the '59 Cadillac, and the three Mustangs Dad had done, Hunter went crazy.

"Are you serious?! That's awesome!" Hunter said.

When I told him about Dad's '64 Mustang under the tarp on the side of the garage, I thought he was going to have a heart attack.

He asked what Dad was going to do with the Mustang, and I told him that my dad always said he had big plans for that car—whatever that meant.

Then Hunter told me his dad always <u>says</u> they'll rebuild a car together someday, but Hunter said, "I bet we won't. He's always too busy working to do anything cool and fun like rebuild a car."

Hunter should just be glad his dad wore a suit every day and had a regular job.

Hunter told me he'd see me later, and as he pedaled away, I stood wondering if the other boys could be right about Hunter because it seemed like he had just stopped by to be nice.

WRITING EXERCISE: Write a riddle poem.

Writing Format—RIDDLE POEM: A creative question used to entertain.

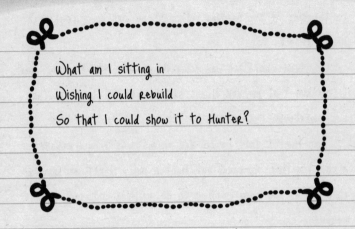

What am I sitting in
Wishing I could rebuild
So that I could show it to Hunter?

Answer: Dad's '64 Mustang parked on the side of the garage.

WRITING EXERCISE: Life Events Journal

I rode my bike to the library today to do my schoolwork there instead of doing it at home. I needed a break from you-know-who. I told him I had to do research for a social studies project. He just smiled like he was the proudest parent of an overachieving homeschooler. For someone so smart, Dad can be really dense sometimes.

Because I'd left, I didn't have to help Dad with the transmission job he was working on. I was glad. Why should I help him all the time when he may have ruined my only chance to find out more about Mom?

On my way home, I turned down my street early so that I could ride by Hunter's house. I knew I probably wouldn't have the guts to stop, but maybe I could wave and say hi to him if he was outside. When I got close, I slowed down, and I noticed Hunter was out in his garage. He was crouched down on the floor with his back to the driveway. As I got closer, I saw him throw something at the garbage can. Whatever it was made a loud thud and clanged to the floor. It sounded almost like a hammer or something. I stood behind some bushes by the curb with my bike and watched. I couldn't believe what I saw. Hunter was wiping his eyes. Hunter was crying.

A few weeks ago I never would've believed it. But now that Hunter wasn't with Evan all the time, it wasn't as hard to believe.

Hunter was actually pretty nice. And a teeny-tiny part of me couldn't help but hope that maybe Hunter might actually like me, especially after the way he stopped by the other day. Not that it really mattered because he'd never be able to let anyone else know if he did.

What did matter was that Hunter was a <u>terrible</u> mechanic. Definitely the worst in the class.

I didn't want Hunter to know I saw him crying, so I made some noise. I waited a minute. Gave him some time to stop crying. Then I hopped on my bike and rode partway up the driveway.

"Hi, Hunter," I called. "What's going on?" I tried to sound like I had no idea what he was doing.

"I'm trying to put the piston into my engine block," he said without turning around.

I asked him if he wanted some help, and I was so glad when he said yes.

First, we worked on putting the connecting rod onto the crankshaft. I'd helped Hunter lots of times before, but here in the garage by ourselves, without the other boys, it felt different.

While I held the piston in place, our hands touched. I wondered if Hunter noticed. And if he did notice, I wondered what he thought.

Then Hunter said something. Something that surprised me more than if he'd punched me in the nose.

"You're lucky, Ratchet."

Me? Lucky?

"Your dad taught you all this cool stuff. I bet you could build anything. My dad doesn't even know what a screwdriver is."

Hunter didn't know what he was talking about. Hunter didn't know how good he had it. Hunter didn't know that if he had a dad like mine he would want him to trade in his screwdriver for a suit any day.

WRITING EXERCISE: Poetry

They say a picture is worth a thousand words,

But sometimes a few words can tell a lot more.

More than a thousand pictures.

A picture is only what you see,

But words can describe

What you hear,

And smell,

And taste.

But most importantly what you feel.

Not what you feel when you touch something,

But how you feel on the inside

When something touches you.

WRITING EXERCISE: Choose a word and write a definition poem about it.

Writing Format—DEFINITION POETRY: Poetry that creatively defines a word or an idea.

A FRIEND

Someone
You're happy to see,
Who's happy to see you.
Someone
You like for who they are
Not just for what they can do for you.
Hunter.
(I hope.)

WRITING EXERCISE: Life Events Journal

Dad was gone for a long time last night. A big city council meeting about Moss Tree Park. AGAIN.

I was sitting in the built-in window seat of the new bay window trying to rub lotion into my rough, calloused hands. The skin was so dry and cracked it was like rubbing oil into cement.

I could finally see out the front window. Replacing the glass was only <u>one</u> of the many jobs Dad needed to do in our current "Handyman Special," and he'd finally done it. I could see through the window for the first time ever because I'd just cleaned the new glass.

After sitting there for a while (I was actually waiting to see if Hunter's mom walked by. Hoping to get a look at what she was wearing), I laid back on the cushion, but when I did, the cushion slid to one side. I got up to straighten it and saw hinges. I realized the window seat opened up like a chest. When I lifted the lid, there it was—a tan metal lockbox. It might as well have been gold. My heart pumped like a piston in a race car because I knew what had to be inside. It <u>had</u> to be the stuff from the mystery box.

I lifted the box out of the window seat and set it down on the floor, ready to finally see what was inside, but I looked at the clock. Dad would be home any minute. I'd have to figure out how to get it open later.

WRITING EXERCISE: Poetry

Funny how finding the lockbox
Helps me find a way to
Forgive Dad for something
He hadn't really done.
I feel my heart's door
Becoming hinged
Again.
So that maybe
I might be able
To open it again sometime.
Maybe sometime soon.

WRITING EXERCISE: Freewriting

"The proper tool for the proper job," is what Dad always says. A flathead screwdriver is not the proper tool to open a lockbox, but when you don't have the key to a box you want to open—a box you need to open, you have no choice—you try to pick the lock, but it's impossible, so you have to find the proper tool—the key.

My mission: to find the lockbox key. I will stop at nothing to find it.

WRITING EXERCISE: Write a friendly letter to someone you haven't spoken to in a while.

Writing Format—FRIENDLY LETTER: An informal letter to a friend or a relative.

Dear Mom,

Even though I don't remember what it was like when you were here, I feel like something's missing now that you're gone. Like the feeling you have when you get your hair cut real short after having it long. You keep touching your neck and the back of your head wondering if you'll ever get used to how different it feels. I don't think I'll ever get used to how different it feels without you.

Dad takes good care of me. But a dad is not the same as a mom. It's like the difference between riding in a beat-up old Jeep instead of a brand-new fancy car. Both can take you where you want to go, but the ride just isn't the same. Because having a mom would make all the difference in the world.

I found the box that (I think) has some of your things in it. I'm hoping I'll find out more about you when I open it. Maybe if I know more about you, I could be more like you. Being like you might make me miss you just a little bit less.

Love,

Ratchet (Rachel)

P.S. Did Dad call me Ratchet when you were alive?

(If Dad read this, I bet he'd be sad.)

WRITING EXERCISE: Freewriting

Maybe it was the thought of that lockbox locked up tight inside the bay window seat. Maybe it was my heart wanting so badly to forgive Dad and give him a second chance. Maybe it was the growing ache inside me for something.

But it didn't matter what it was that made me ask the question. It didn't matter because Dad said, "Ratchet, leave well enough alone," when I asked him about the lockbox.

"But, Dad—" I started to say, but never finished because he interrupted with, "It's nothing that concerns you. You hear me?"

And I felt my anger closing the door again on forgiveness.

WRITING EXERCISE: Poetry

The mute button

Has been pressed.

Again.

Every day

Life is still happening—

Eating meals,

Fixing cars,

Sneaking off

To build go-carts

With the boys,

But the sound

Between Dad and me

Is turned off.

I'm not sure if he

Even notices.

Maybe

It isn't an accident

When the jack slips

And Dad screams,

"JACK IT UP!

JACK IT UP!"

And I do,

Right away!

But it's too late.

Blood is everywhere.

Dad's thumb,

Crushed.

I'd been lowering a car with the floor jack. To rest it on the jack stand. Something I'd done hundreds of times. Even so, Dad had reminded me, like he always does, "Take it slow...Take it slow..." And I did take it slow. At first. But then something happened. Did my hand slip? Did the car slip?

Or did I go too fast? On purpose? Because I was mad. So
mad at Dad.

But now I see him

Holding his hand,

The hand that knows how to

Tighten bolts and loosen screws,

Squeeze pliers and connect hoses,

Remove gaskets and stretch oil rings into place

Without even looking.

The hand that knows how to do everything.

He's holding it out like it's on fire.

And I'm crying,

"Dad, Dad,

I'm sorry,

I'm sorry!"

"Hurry!

Get the first aid kit!"

And I do.

Ripping it open,

fumbling through it,

finding some gauze,

And watching my hands shake

As I unwrap it.

"Ratchet, it's okay.

It was an accident.

Don't worry,"

Dad says as the white gauze turns bright red

As blood seeps into its woven strands.

And now my tears

Come from somewhere else.

A place so deep,

A place so deep

I never even knew it was there.

And I feel myself breaking from the inside.

Later,

Dad's stitches

Hold the skin

Between his thumb

And index finger together,

But it tears my insides apart.

Seeing it

When he changes the bandage

Makes my chest

feel tighter than Dad's skin looks.

And my head throbs every time I think about what the doctor said. "Stay out of the garage for at least a week. This thing gets infected, and you'll <u>really</u> be sorry."

I am much sorrier than that already.

WRITING EXERCISE: Define a vocabulary word with a situational example.

VOCABULARY WORD—<u>Remorse</u>: feeling sorry or regretful about something that has happened or about something you have caused to happen.

I knew why I was sorry, but for some reason, Dad seemed sorry too. I'm not sure about what, but he told me to tell the boys it was okay to build the go-carts in our garage.

"That way you can use our tools when you help them," Dad said.

Somehow he had known all along that I had been helping the boys. It made me think he might know other things too: like how bad I felt about dropping the car. It made me feel good to think he knew that, but if he somehow knew that, did it mean he knew there was a chance the accident hadn't really been an accident? If he knew that, I knew my sorry would never be enough.

WRITING EXERCISE: Life Events Journal

Dad couldn't work in the garage, so he was inside making phone calls. Talking to anyone who would listen to him go on and on about Moss Tree Park.

Dad had found paperwork on Herman Moss's other parks. He thought that was proof that there had to be the same paperwork for Moss Tree Park, but something— something not so ethical, as Dad put it—had happened to the Moss Tree Park paperwork. Dad kept telling people that "someone," probably that crooked excuse we have for a mayor, and his buddy, Pretty Boy Eddie, decided to take matters into their own hands because they're so greedy and all they think about is money. Of course, the city council members, who are all friends with both of them, didn't see it that way.

Dad kept saying in this weird ominous voice, "You can run,

but you can't hide, especially not from the Good Lord. The truth is going to come out."

Every time I looked at the big bandage on Dad's hand, I felt like his voice was for me. I couldn't listen to that voice of doom anymore, so I was out sweeping the garage. Singing along with a Beatles song trying to let the lyrics fill up my head.

Then I heard someone else singing too. I turned around, and there was Hunter.

"I thought I was the only one who knew all the words to that song," he said.

I didn't know what he was doing here.

"I know we don't have another class until the weekend," he said, "but would you help me figure out how to get the keepers on the valves in my engine?"

It took me one nanosecond to say yes.

I yelled inside to Dad that I was going to Hunter's.

Hunter and I spent the next hour in his garage taking things apart, and step-by-step, putting them back together. Once we got it all back together, Hunter looked as happy as I felt. But that wasn't the best part. The best part was that our hands touched three times.

WRITING EXERCISE: Use dialogue to keep the action moving in a scene.

When we finished working in Hunter's garage, we used the hose on the driveway to wash our hands.

"Thanks for all your help, Ratchet," Hunter said.

"No problem," is what I said out loud, but what I was saying in my head was, "Are you kidding? I should be thanking you for asking me to help."

That's when my hand slipped, and I squirted water right in Hunter's face.

"Hey!" he said, acting all mad.

"Sorry," I said.

I couldn't believe I'd gotten him so wet.

Hunter wiped the water out of his eyes, but then he laughed, grabbed the end of the hose, and pointed it right at me. I yanked it away from him and sprayed him again. He ran to the front yard and turned on the other hose lying in the bushes.

"Take that!" he yelled as he aimed and fired.

"Oh, yeah," I said as I picked up a nearby garbage can lid and held it up like a shield.

"Not gonna work!" Hunter yelled, squirting his hose high into the air so it arched like a fountain over the top of my shield.

"I'm soaked!" I screamed as the water poured down on me. I dropped the lid and squirted my hose right at Hunter, drenching him from head to toe.

"What about me? Do I look dry?" Hunter asked.

Both of us kept squirting our hoses and running around trying to dodge the spray raining down on us.

When we were out of breath, and there wasn't a dry spot on either one of us, we called a truce.

Just then Hunter's mom came out on the driveway.

"Hunter, is that any way to treat a girl?" she asked.

"Oh, Mom," Hunter groaned.

As I walked home leaving a trail of water on the sidewalk, all I could think was I hope it's exactly how you treat a girl if you want her to be your friend.

WRITING EXERCISE: Life Events Journal

Dad had not only agreed to let the boys work in our garage, but he said he'd help them when he had time. I thought working with Dad again would help soothe my guilt, but the first thing Dad did when the boys got there was hold up his bandaged hand. I couldn't look at anybody.

"Doesn't matter how good you are with the tools or how much you know about engines. What really matters?"

The boys all mumbled the word "safety" because the safety rules were the first thing Dad had taught them, and now thanks to me, he had a great excuse to review them.

"Accidents like this can happen to anyone, anywhere, anytime."

As Dad told the story of me "accidentally" lowering the jack too fast, I felt as if the weight of a semitrailer truck filled with the heaviest load it could possibly carry inched closer and closer to my chest getting ready to crush my soul.

WRITING EXERCISE: Life Events Journal

Today out in the driveway, Dad had all the boys in class try to start their engines. Everyone's engine worked except Hunter's. I didn't know why his wasn't working because I'd helped him with so much of it. Hunter tried and tried and tried. After the sixth time, he mumbled, "I gotta go," and walked down the street toward home. I wondered if he was crying again. I couldn't run after him. I wanted to. But I didn't know if Hunter wanted me to. I didn't even know if Hunter thought we were friends. And even if he did, I didn't know if he wanted anyone else to know.

If Dad were clued into more than just global warming, he might have realized that I would want to go after Hunter. But, since Dad's head is always somewhere in the disappearing ozone layer, he told Jason to go get him, and I missed my chance.

Jason came back by himself. He told Dad that Hunter just wanted to go home. So while the rest of the kids high-fived one another about their engines working, Hunter

walked home by himself probably feeling like a failure. I
wanted to find a way to make him feel better. Because I
didn't want to fail as a friend.

If Mom were here I could ask her what I should do.

These are the kinds of things moms know.

Instead I sat wondering if Hunter even wanted my help.

I didn't have to wonder very long about Hunter. He came back after all the boys left. He told Dad and me that the other day when I'd helped him in his garage, he had been so excited about getting his engine together that after I left, he took the whole thing apart again so that he could put it back together by himself. Obviously Hunter hadn't learned very much because his engine was a mess.

When we looked at it together, I couldn't believe how many things were wrong. He hadn't even lined up the timing marks on the camshaft. There's no way an engine will run if you forget to do this. How could he have missed that? He also had the oil rings and one compression ring in the wrong place. Half the things he did didn't even make any sense.

"Well, I've got some phone calls to make," Dad said. "So Ratchet will have to help you."

And Dad went inside, leaving me with Hunter and his messed-up small engine. Maybe Dad's head wasn't as far up in the ozone layer as I thought.

At first Hunter was real quiet, and the only sound was Dad's oldies station playing in the background. I think Hunter was embarrassed about needing so much help again, but by the time we got the engine apart and were ready to put it back together again, Hunter seemed to be in a better mood. And by the time we were putting in the spark plug, we were singing to the radio.

Hunter sang the chorus of "Hang on Sloopy" into the end of a wrench.

I tapped out the beat with a screwdriver and some pliers. And we both laughed.

I knew Hunter had lots of friends and probably goofed around like this all the time, but for me, this moment was a dream come true.

We finally got Hunter's small engine running. It was the kind of thing Dad and I did every day; but for Hunter, this was <u>his</u> dream come true.

WRITING EXERCISE: Write a memo to a group of people you know.

Writing Format—MEMO: A brief written message that asks and answers questions, gives instructions, describes work done, and reminds people about deadlines and meetings.

A few days later, Dad reviewed the safety rules again, and then he handed out this memo.

Note: Since Dad still can't use his hand to write, he told me what to write for this memo. So technically, I'm cheating. I think the word is "plagiarism." But I'm sure, if by chance, Dad actually reads this, he won't care.

DAY: SATURDAY

TO: GO-CART CLASS

FROM: MR. VANCE/AKA RACCOON DOG

SUBJECT: ENGINE TEST NEXT SATURDAY

1. You must know:
   * Safety rules

- * Names of tools
- * How to use them
- * Names of engine parts
- * How to take engine apart
- * How to put engine back together

2. Ratchet and I have taught it. You've practiced it. Now we test it. And, hopefully, you prove it.

3. You pass the test: We all go to the junkyard to find parts. You build your car. And race at Moss Tree Park.

4. You don't pass the test: No trip to the junkyard. No building a car. No race at Moss Tree Park.

5. Today we're going on a field trip to Moss Tree Park. In order to have the race, we have to save the park. If we keep the park clean, we have more chance of saving it. Fill up one plastic bag with garbage, then go home and study.

WRITING EXERCISE: Life Events Journal

Dad handed out the engine test memo. The boys complained about picking up trash. Then moaned and groaned "pretending" to be worried about the test, but Hunter freaked out. He was NOT pretending. He said he'll NEVER be able to pass the test. The worst part is he's probably right. He still doesn't know a crankshaft from a piston. And I keep wondering, How can that be?

How in the world will he ever pass the test?

WRITING EXERCISE: Poetry

Scattered among the leaves and twigs,
Resting in the grass and moss,
Lazy people's trash.
Plastic bottles, empty bags,
Straws, and tin cans.

Rowdy boys
And one quiet girl
Fill up plastic bags.
But the girl finds
Something else left behind
From a long time ago
In the bark of a tree.
Carved letters leave
A mark of love.
Just one more reason
This park and these trees
Should be saved.

H. M. + A.W.
my love is as deep
as these roots

WRITING EXERCISE: Life Events Journal

Today Dad sent me up to Gas Gulp to fill up our gasoline container. He needed it to test an old riding mower someone had dropped off for him to fix.

He wasn't supposed to be working in the garage yet, but he said, "You know what they say—idle hands means an idle mind, and the Good Lord gave me too many brains for that."

I was thinking the Good Lord should've given Dad the brains to listen to the doctor.

Marty, the owner of Gas Gulp, really wasn't supposed to sell gas to a kid, but Dad had fixed his car for free a bunch of times, so Marty would've even delivered the gas to our house if Dad wanted him to.

I liked running errands for Dad because it got me out of the garage, but my timing was really bad. I was filling up the container when Hunter and Evan showed up on their bikes. Probably to buy candy. Marty sold candy bars real cheap, to drum up more business.

He always said, "The way to a man's wallet is through his

gas tank. The way to get him to fill up that tank at your station? Give him a reason to stop. Candy bars are a good reason, and cheap ones are an even better one."

That's why Gas Gulp was always more crowded than Pump It Up at the other end of town. Pump It Up was the station Pretty Boy Eddie owned, so Dad never went there.

Seeing Hunter would've been fine. Nice even. But he was with Evan, so I wasn't sure what would happen. I hadn't seen Evan since I'd started helping the boys with their go-carts.

I knew there was no chance that Hunter and Evan wouldn't see me, so I braced myself for Evan's insults. At the same time, I tried not to think about how it would hurt even more now if Hunter went right along with Evan and his mean jokes.

"Look, Hunter," Evan said. "Now Ratchet's a gas girl."

Hunter got off his bike but didn't look at me.

I concentrated on the numbers as they flipped on the gas pump.

Evan made some crack about me cleaning the gas station bathrooms as he kicked down his kickstand.

Then I heard, "Shut up."

I whipped my head around to look at Hunter. He was staring right at Evan, and he had just told him to shut up.

"What?" asked Evan.

"I said, shut up," Hunter said louder.

"You're kidding, right?" Evan said.

"No," Hunter said, throwing his leg back over his bike. "I'm not kidding, and I gotta go."

And Hunter was gone before Evan could say anything else.

I turned back to the gas pump and finished filling my container, then put it in the milk crate on the back of my bike and took off. I never even looked back to see what Evan did.

It didn't matter.

The only thing that mattered was what Hunter had just done.

It mattered a lot.

WRITING EXERCISE: Write a list poem about a task you must do.

HELPING HUNTER GET READY FOR THE BIG TEST

Make flash cards.

Put labels on tools.

Put labels on engine parts.

Make a diagram of an engine.

Make a four-stroke cycle poster.

Review everything with Hunter.

Make up a quiz.

Give Hunter the quiz.

Cross my fingers...

WRITING EXERCISE: Freewriting

Dad's working like crazy trying to catch up on all the repairs that got backed up because of the accident. I hate to see him have to work with his hand all bandaged up—it makes everything harder, so I'm helping him even more than usual.

I feel so guilty when I see that big white bandage, but as the guilt turns over and over in my mind like a combination wrench, I find my anger on the other end of it—my anger at Dad about the mystery box—the anger that caused this whole thing to happen.

I still don't know what's in the box, and Dad won't tell me.

I don't know where the key is to the box, so I still haven't opened it.

It feels like my guilt and anger make the big empty space inside me get bigger and emptier every day.

WRITING EXERCISE: Freewriting

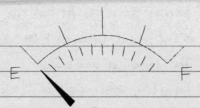

Yesterday we changed a fan belt and a water pump and did a brake job. All in one day. And to use a corny pun—I'm running out of gas. As Dad's hand gets better, my guilt does too, but my anger gets worse. Does Dad really think he can tell me to leave well enough alone and believe for a minute that I'll forget all about the box that obviously has Mom's stuff in it?

So I've decided not to do any of my homeschool assignments. I'm supposed to be a full-time student. Not a full-time mechanic. If Dad's going to overwork me in the garage and not answer a really important question, then I'm going to do whatever I want when he finally lets me take a "break" (as he calls it) to study. I'm doing my journal writing and some language arts assignments (only the ones that look like fun) because that IS a break. Making a time line of important world events for social studies or doing long division with remainders for math ISN'T.

Besides, with all the extra time I'm spending helping Hunter study for the go-cart test, I don't even have time for my assignments. The worst part is I feel like Hunter hasn't learned a thing. Today better be the day that "the fuel gets to the engine," as Dad puts it. Otherwise I don't know what I'm going to do. Test day will be here soon.

But at least I'm getting something out of it. We've studied at Hunter's house a couple of times. It's been great! His mom is always floating around doing nice things. Smiling. Bringing us juice boxes. (Hunter rolled his eyes when she did that. Said his mom was embarrassing him. He doesn't know what embarrassment is until he's lived with my dad.)

Yesterday she even made butter cookies with sprinkles on them. (Hunter didn't mind when she did that.) They were even better than the chocolate chip cookies she brought over when we fixed her car. She gave me a whole bunch to take home. Since I'm so mad at Dad I was thinking about hiding them when I got home so I could eat them all myself. But when I saw Dad on the garage floor still lying on his back underneath someone's Jeep changing the oil, I decided Hunter's mom's butter cookies were something Dad really needed. The same way I really needed someone like Hunter to be my friend.

WRITING EXERCISE: Poetry

HUNTER'S MOM	HUNTER
Turquoise everything	Fun
Sundress	Being together
flip-flops	frustrating
Ponytail holder	Studying together
Earrings	He
Even her smile	Doesn't
Is	Remember
Bright blue	Anything

WRITING EXERCISE: Poetry

Back to the
Goodwill store
for matching
Anything.
Come close with the
Lime green tank top.
(Only a small brown stain.)
Dark green cutoffs.
(Missing a button.)
Olive green plastic flip-flops.
(Almost new.)
And a white scrunchie.
(Still in the package.)
When I stand at the mirror
I look better than usual,
But not as good as I had hoped.
Haven't really
Created
My own style
Yet.

WRITING EXERCISE: Do-Over Assignment:
MEMO

(I'm writing my own memo this time.)

DAY: WEDNESDAY
TO: RATCHET
FROM: RATCHET
SUBJECT: STUDYING WITH HUNTER

After studying for four days:

1. Hunter knows the names of almost all the tools, but still looks
    like a preschooler with a toy tool kit when he uses them.
2. He doesn't know the names of hardly any engine parts.
3. He can take the engine apart but still has no idea how to put
    it back together.
4. He couldn't explain the four-stroke cycle if his life depended on it.
5. As a mechanic, Hunter is as hopeless as a spark plug
    without a spark.

WRITING EXERCISE: Write a personal
response to a well-known proverb.

JEWISH PROVERB:

"A mother understands what a child does not say."

RATCHET'S RESPONSE:

Dad doesn't notice

My almost matching clothes.

My ponytail looking neater

Than usual.

My waiting for Hunter to get home

From school.

A MOM,

My mom,

Would've noticed all of this

And even more.

She would've noticed

I was excited,

Even a little bit nervous.

She would've noticed

How hard I was trying
To make a good impression.
She would've noticed
How important it was for me
To have a friend.
And she would've noticed
That having a boy like Hunter
Pay attention,
Really pay attention
Is a _really_ big deal.

WRITING EXERCISE: Poetry

Hunter doesn't notice my clothes.

But

We don't study.

We play video games.

Hanging out like real friends.

It makes me feel as good on the inside

As I had hoped to look on the outside.

WRITING EXERCISE: Write a realistic one-act play.

Writing Format—A PLAY: The stage representation of a scene or a story.

Scene: The garage. Tools and engine parts scattered everywhere. Oldies music playing in the background. Ratchet points to the intake valve on a small engine.

RATCHET: What's this?

Hunter looks puzzled as if he's seeing an engine for the first time. He sighs.

HUNTER: I don't know.

RATCHET: How can you not know?! We've been over this a thousand times!

Hunter shakes his head.

HUNTER: I've been studying all week long, and I still don't know half this stuff. I don't have a chance!

Hunter buries his head in his hands. Ratchet stands awkwardly shifting her weight from one foot to the other wondering if Hunter's crying. The song "Daydream

Believer" starts to play in the background. Hunter looks
up and half smiles.

HUNTER: "Cheer up, Sleepy Jean..."

Hunter and Ratchet both burst out laughing as they pretend
to play air keyboard for the rest of the song. Finally, they
fall on the floor of the garage laughing as a new song comes
on the radio.

RATCHET: I've got it! I know how you're going to pass
the test.

Ratchet grabs a clipboard and a pencil. Hunter looks confused.

RATCHET: What are your five favorite oldies songs?

HUNTER: What?

RATCHET: Just tell me. What are they?

HUNTER: "Spirit in the Sky," "Jailhouse Rock," "I Heard It
Through the Grapevine," "Born to Be Wild," and "Proud Mary."

RATCHET: Now all we have to do is change the lyrics.

HUNTER: What in the world are you talking about?

RATCHET: We'll write new words to the old songs. Good-
bye, love, heartbreak, and tears. Hello, spark plug, gasket,
and flywheel. You're going to sing your way to an A."

The scene fades as Ratchet grabs a clipboard from the workbench.
Hunter looks over her shoulder as she begins to write.

WRITING EXERCISE: Freewriting

Since I'm not doing many assignments anymore, if Dad asks to see my work, I can flash my language arts notebook at him, and when he sees all this writing, he'll think I'm in the running to be the top homeschool student of the year. It's amazing how someone so in touch with the environment can be so out of touch with reality.

For the last week I've been writing (or I should say rewriting) songs. It's Hunter's only hope. If he remembers the songs, he'll pass the test.

Here's one of my favorites:

"PISTON ROCK"

(To the tune of "Jailhouse Rock" by Elvis Presley)

The piston threw a party in the engine block.

The four-stroke cycle started and things began to rock.

The valve opened up, and fuel and air came in.

The flywheel got excited, and it began to spin.

Let's rock, everybody, let's rock.

Every part in the engine block

Was dancing to the piston rock.

WRITING EXERCISE: Write a ballad.

*Writing Format—*BALLAD: A poem that tells a story.

Sitting at the kitchen table wondering
If Hunter knows enough lyrics to pass the test,
The phone rings and Dad answers it in the garage.
He yells, "Ratchet, bring me my keys!
I gotta go jump someone's car."
I see the keys where they always are up on
the windowsill next to his wallet,
And it hits me—
The key to the lockbox is in Dad's wallet.
It's got to be.
When I pick up the car keys, my hand is so
close to the wallet.
Going into Dad's wallet would be crossing a line.
A line I've never crossed.
The phone rings again startling me, and Dad's

car keys clatter to the floor.

"Forget it!" Dad yells from the garage.

"They just got the car started."

I put the keys back.

My hand touches the wallet, and I watch my

hand pick it up.

I watch like it's someone else's hands

As they unfold the worn leather

And slide open the little zipper that's inside,

And someone else's index finger pokes into the

tiny pocket,

But my finger feels the metal key.

The metal key that I know will open the lockbox.

A thumb and index finger dig it out,

And before I know it the wallet is back on

the windowsill next to the car keys,

And THE key is in my shorts' pocket pressing

into my thigh like it weighs a ton,

And I sit back down at the kitchen table

wondering when I'll have the guts to use it.

WRITING EXERCISE: Life Events Journal

It was dark outside by the time I went out to the garage to see what Dad wanted for supper, and he was lying on the creeper in the middle of the garage floor. His hair was wet with sweat, and his cheeks were bright red. He was just staring at the ceiling.

I asked him if he was okay.

He didn't answer, so I went over and knelt down next to him.

"Ratchet, go get my wallet. I gotta get to the hospital."

I ran inside. My hands shook as I grabbed his wallet off the windowsill. This time it was <u>my</u> hands holding the wallet, and they were trying to save Dad. I hurried back out to the garage.

Dad asked me to help him up, and when I touched his arm, he felt like an overheated engine.

I asked him what was wrong.

"Don't know. I've just gotta get to the hospital."

I asked if he could even drive.

"I'll manage. You better come with me."

He started up the Rabbit, and the fried chicken smell made me want to throw up. Dad hunched over the steering wheel and accelerated toward the hospital.

WRITING EXERCISE: Poetry

Sitting next to Dad in the hospital room.

His IV drips slowly,

But my tears pour

Until a doctor

finally tells me

He'll be all right.

"Are you sure?"

I keep asking.

And yes,

Everyone keeps saying,

So my tears slow to a drip

And keep time with the IV.

The infection happened

Because Dad

Worked in the garage

Too soon.

Teeny-tiny germs

Seeped through the bandage

And sneaked into Dad's hand,

Swam into his veins,

Spread throughout his whole body,

So with each drip of the IV

I silently apologize to Dad

Over and over again

Because my anger

Had already hurt him

On the outside,

And now it was hurting him

On the inside too.

SORRY :-(

WRITING EXERCISE: Poetry

Awake
   My neck stiff
      My mind foggy.
         Where am I?
A dim hospital room
With the TV muted
And Dad sleeping in the bed.
His cheeks already looking
Their normal color.

My legs stick to the plastic recliner I lay in.
I stretch to get more comfortable
And I feel the key.
The small silver key
   That I secretly dug out of
      Dad's beat-up, worn-out wallet
         While he was outside
Lying on the garage floor.

WRITING EXERCISE: Life Events Journal

"I thought the Good Lord might've been calling me home yesterday," Dad said when he woke up. "Glad he's letting me stick around for a while."

I thought I had used up all my tears, but when Dad said that I knew I had more.

Later Dad sent me home in a cab and said he'd be home as soon as these crazy doctors let him go. I knew Dad well enough to know that he felt grateful for the crazy doctors who probably saved his life. The only person who felt more grateful than Dad was me.

Dad told me if he wasn't home by the time the boys came for class that I should give them the engine test, which was lying on the workbench.

I didn't go down to the hospital lobby until I found out from a nurse what Dad needed to do at home. Antibiotics every day and no working with his hand for two weeks.

The antibiotics would be easy, but the rest would be impossible.

WRITING EXERCISE: Freewriting

The boys left after taking their test. Dad wasn't home from the hospital yet. I still had the key in my pocket. Should I use it? I knew Dad didn't want me to, and I'd already hurt him so much, but didn't I have the right to know what was inside the box?

As I slid the key into the keyhole, that deep down place inside me felt like something was finally going to happen.

THE MYSTERY BOX

AFTER TURNING THE KEY, I LIFT THE LID AND
I PEEK INSIDE TO SEE THE PHOTOS OF MOM
AND ME WHEN I WAS BORN. AND ME LYING
NEXT TO MOM IN BED. AND MOM HOLDING
MY HANDS AND HELPING ME WALK. SO MANY
PHOTOS OF US. MORE STUFF IN THE BOX. BUT
I SMELL FRIED CHICKEN. DAD IS HOME SO I
LOCK THE BOX AND HIDE IT AGAIN FOR NOW.

WRITING EXERCISE: Freewriting

A question without an answer:

Why would Dad not want me to see what's in the box?

WRITING EXERCISE: Write a postcard greeting.

Writing Format—POSTCARD: Form of writing used to stay in touch or send a short message.

To the Town of Blainesfield,

Green light for go-carts. Everyone passed the test. Even Hunter.
But Moss Tree Park won't be green.
Dad gets an A for effort, but a big fat f for results.
No racing flags or starting lines. Instead tags on trees to cut down.
Bulldozers, not go-carts, will tear up the track.

Sadly Yours,
Ratchet

.... Town of Blainesfield
....
....
....

WRITING EXERCISE: Freewriting

I wonder sometimes if the Good Lord realizes everything Dad tries to do to help him because sometimes it sure doesn't seem like it. Dad's thumb getting crushed, another trip to the hospital, and now we're losing the park. After all Dad's done?

I'm still mad at Dad about him keeping the box from me, but it sure doesn't seem like he deserves all this.

Thankfully Dad is an optimistic environmentalist. I guess that's one advantage to thinking the Good Lord is on your side.

He says he's not giving up on Moss Tree Park. Not yet anyway. He still hopes to find some way to prove that Mr. Moss never wanted a strip mall on his land.

So everyone's still building their go-carts. I was worried. If there was no race, maybe there would be no go-carts. And that might mean there would be no Hunter. I'm glad Dad's not giving up.

WRITING EXERCISE: Life Events Journal

I watched the public access channel tonight. I had to. Everyone in the go-cart class went to see Dad. Dad assigned it for homework because he was scheduled to talk about Moss Tree Park at the city council meeting that aired live at 7 p.m. Maybe his last chance before the bulldozers moved in.

It's hard to sit in your living room watching your own dad yell at people who look a lot smarter than him. I know Dad's smart. But the way he dresses and talks makes everyone shake their heads and roll their eyes as if to say, "This guy CAN'T be for real."

I guess all the boys in Dad's class wanted extra credit because they didn't just show up at the meeting, they held a big sign that said, "Listen to Mr. Vance! Give Moss Tree Park a Chance!" It was kind of a clever saying, but the sign looked dumb. Whoever wrote the letters didn't sketch it out with pencil first so the letters got smaller and smaller because they ran out of room. Still, I couldn't believe they'd all shown up.

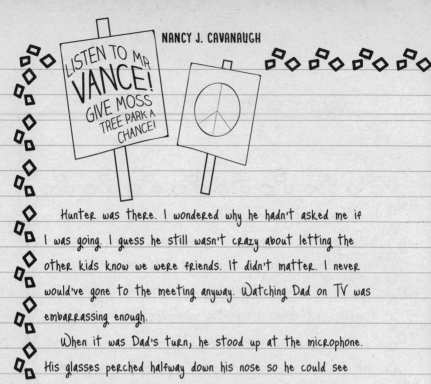

NANCY J. CAVANAUGH

LISTEN TO MR VANCE! GIVE MOSS TREE PARK A CHANCE!

Hunter was there. I wondered why he hadn't asked me if I was going. I guess he still wasn't crazy about letting the other kids know we were friends. It didn't matter. I never would've gone to the meeting anyway. Watching Dad on TV was embarrassing enough.

When it was Dad's turn, he stood up at the microphone. His glasses perched halfway down his nose so he could see over them to give the city council members his I'm-so-disgusted-with-you-people-I-don't-know-what-to-do look. He wore his T-shirt that said, "In the Land of the Blind, the One-Eyed Man is King." (I don't even know what that means, but he saved this shirt for the <u>really</u> big meetings.)

He started by saying, "I have no choice. I've got to rant and rave because you people don't respect reason, and you stare truth in the face and scoff at it. You're idiots!"

I wondered what all the parents of the boys from Dad's class were thinking when Dad called everyone idiots. I hoped Hunter's mom wasn't watching.

"Stealing from the future and disrespecting the past. Do you really think you'll be heroes to your children when you ruin every last thing the Good Lord has given us?"

The cameraman kept going back and forth from Dad to the boys holding the sign. And every time Dad finished a sentence, the boys clapped.

"History is the architect, and you people don't listen to logic."

That was the problem with Dad. He always talked like this. Why couldn't he just say things in plain English? How about, "Save the park," or "We need more green space," or "Let's not forget the legacy of Herman Moss"?

But no, Dad had to go on and on with his strange way of saying everything.

He continued, "Oh, I love suburbia"—I could tell by his voice that he had saved his most sarcastic remark for the very end—"they cut down the trees and then name streets after them."

It was a wonder they even let Dad have a turn at the microphone.

(If Dad read this, he would beam with pride at his performance.)

WRITING EXERCISE: Life Events Journal

Dad reminded me today that I better get busy with all my homeschool work for this quarter. It's almost time for him to send my final assignments and tests to the homeschool evaluation committee. I knew this day was coming. I have tons of stuff left to do. I don't know why I did this to myself. I stopped doing my work because I was mad at Dad, but all I've done is punish myself.

My final assignment in language arts is a real paper. A persuasive essay. Yuck! Besides that, I have to write a modern day fairy tale, do another summary of a newspaper article, and make another graphic organizer.

Then I'm going to have to figure out what's due in all the other subjects. I haven't opened any of my books for weeks.

If I don't get my work done, next quarter Dad will be on me like an oil ring on a piston.

YIKES!

I haven't seen Hunter since Dad's TV appearance. Now I'm really starting to wonder if he only used me. Maybe I was just someone who could help him get what he wanted—a passing grade on the test and a chance to build a go-cart. I'm telling myself it doesn't matter, but deep down it does.

I'm trying to concentrate on my assignments, but I'd rather be doing work for Dad, especially since he's got three cars out in the garage that he can't even work on because of his hand. Dad won't let me out there until I have some of my assignments ready to send in. I never thought I liked working on cars until I had to sit at the kitchen table for days at a time without so much as picking up a screwdriver.

The worst part: Hunter hasn't stopped by once.

WRITING EXERCISE: Life Events Journal

Dad got a call this morning. Some guy's car broke down so he left to go help him. I made him promise he'd only look at it and not fix it.

As soon as I heard the Vegetable Rabbit squeal out of the garage, I headed straight for the mystery box before the fried chicken smell was even gone. I took out all the things I'd already seen to get to the new stuff.

I found more photos. Most were of Mom and Dad—one on their wedding day, another of them at the beach with the sunset behind them, one with them on a motorcycle. I could tell they weren't just smiling for the camera. Their smiles were from somewhere deep down. They looked really happy. I stared at each picture for a long time. Trying to see something. Something that would tell me more about Mom and Dad. Something I never knew.

I also found birth certificates for Mom, Dad, and me, and two pieces of folded-up paper that looked like letters. Before I had the chance to read them I smelled Dad coming,

☆

so I put everything back into the box and locked it. I put it back in the bay window seat and laid the cushion on top.

By the time Dad got inside, I was sitting at the kitchen table doing division with remainders.

WRITING EXERCISE: Freewriting

Now the question without an answer gets even harder to answer:
Why would Dad not want me to see what's in the box?

WHY WHY WHY WHY WHY WHY WHY WHY WHY WHY
WHY WHY WHY WHY WHY WHY WHY WHY WHY WHY
WHY WHY WHY WHY WHY WHY WHY WHY WHY WHY
WHY WHY WHY WHY WHY WHY WHY WHY WHY WHY
WHY WHY WHY WHY WHY WHY WHY WHY WHY WHY
WHY WHY WHY WHY WHY WHY WHY WHY WHY WHY
WHY   !?   !?   WHY WHY WHY WHY WHY
WHY   WHY WHY WHY WHY WHY
WHY   WHY WHY WHY WHY WHY
WHY   WHY WHY WHY WHY WHY
WHY WHY   !?   WHY WHY WHY WHY WHY

WRITING EXERCISE: Write a persuasive essay.

Writing Format—PERSUASIVE ESSAY: An essay written to convince readers to agree with your opinion.

(Rough Draft)

My dad ~~tries to make~~ (wants) people to care about global warming. I think it would be easier if he just tried to ~~to get~~ (convince) people to care about trees.

Too much carbon dioxide is the biggest cause of global warming. Cutting down trees ~~puts~~ (is what puts too much) carbon dioxide into the atmosphere. Since we can't <u>see</u> carbon dioxide or <u>feel</u> the global warming, nobody notices it's happening.

But if you go to the park on a hot day and you want to cool off, what do you look for? A tree. ~~Because~~ (S)tanding in the shade is the best way to cool off. If we cut down the trees, the shade will be gone. People will notice that.

If we ~~love~~ (destroy) Moss Tree Park just so we can have another strip mall, we'll be losing something we can never get back— lots and lots of trees.

~~Sometimes~~ When when you lose something you can never get back, you aren't ever the same person again. If we lose Moss Tree Park, our neighborhood will never be the same. We'd be losing something REALLY important. Something we ~~can~~ will NEVER get back. And THAT'S a big deal.

Don't think about global warming. Think about the trees. Moss Tree Park should be saved.

(If Dad read this, I'd get an A plus for sure.)

Today I came back from riding my bike to the drugstore. (We ran out of toilet paper. That's the kind of thing a mom would make sure DIDN'T happen, but the kind of thing Dad never pays attention to.) Guess who was in the garage talking to Dad when I got back? Hunter. He barely even noticed me when I parked my bike against the wall. I hadn't seen him in a couple of days and then he came around to see Dad? What was up with that?

You would've thought he was trying to brownnose Dad the way he was listening to him go on and on about Moss Tree Park. I love parks as much as the next guy, but there are other things to talk about. It made me want to go inside and rip up my persuasive essay. I was sick of hearing about trees and parks. Maybe I should write about shopping malls instead.

I wasn't going to stand around being ignored by both Dad and Hunter. I took my bag of toilet paper and walked toward the kitchen door. But then I noticed a blue and white striped gift bag hanging on the doorknob.

I asked what it was, and I saw Hunter looking at me out

of the corner of his eye. I looked inside. A homemade CD. The title was written on the cover in big black letters with one of those fat permanent markers.

GREATEST HITS
FROM THE
GO-CART GARAGE

Lyrics by Ratchet

Vocals sung by Hunter

Hunter and I looked at each other and smiled like we shared the biggest inside joke of the century. Dad kept talking about trees and carbon dioxide, but Hunter wasn't paying attention to him anymore. Hunter walked toward me.

"Thanks. I couldn't've passed without you. I mean without your songs," he said.

I felt like a balloon full of friendship helium ready to float up, up, and away.

WRITING EXERCISE: Poetry

That night in my room

Alone

Listening to Hunter's voice

Sing,

I feel something

Changing.

I had written the songs for

Hunter,

He had made the CD for

Me,

And I finally knew we were

friends.

Having a friend like

Hunter,

Having a friend at

All,

Is really a nice

Change.

Yesterday I felt like I was flying in the clouds full of friendship helium, but today I feel like a big old truck tire. One that's blown apart on the highway so bad that even Dad can't fix it.

I finally read the letters. The ones from the mystery box. I was excited thinking they might be letters Mom wrote to me. But they weren't. Both letters were written to Dad. The first one was from someone named Sandy who must've been Mom's friend. The letter was short, telling Dad how sorry she was that Mom had died. It had been a car accident. I had always known that. Along with the letter from Sandy was the clipping from the obituary section of the paper. I wondered why Sandy had sent it to Dad. Wouldn't Dad have saved his own copy? And I was surprised that mine and Dad's names weren't mentioned in the newspaper.

But that wasn't the letter that blew my tires to kingdom come. The other letter was written a year earlier.

It was from Mom.

To Dad.

About her leaving.

Leaving Dad.

Leaving me.

Mom left us?

How come I didn't remember that?

Mom wrote that she didn't love Dad anymore. She was tired of living in broken-down houses. She was tired of him working all the time and not making enough money. She was tired of him talking about the Good Lord all the time and spending every minute of every day thinking about "saving the world."

It was funny because those were all the things I was tired of. But I hadn't <u>ever</u> once thought of leaving Dad.

WRITING EXERCISE: Freewriting

The question without an answer just got answered.

Why would Dad not want me to see what was in the box?

Turns out Dad had a really good reason—one I never could've imagined.

Now I have another question without an answer:

If I couldn't even imagine the truth, I wonder if that means what I thought was the truth was really only imagined?

WRITING EXERCISE: Poetry

How does a mom

Leave?

How does she

Live

After she's

Left?

How does her

Heart

Not break?

How does she

Write

A letter

Instead of

Staying

To be

A mom?

WRITING EXERCISE: Respond personally to a famous quote.

WHITNEY HOUSTON:

"She's (my mother) my teacher, my advisor, my greatest inspiration."

RATCHET'S RESPONSE:

What could a mom who left

Teach me to think

Except that

I wasn't worth sticking around for.

What could a mom who left

Advise me to do

Except to

Quit when things don't go my way.

What could a mom who left

Inspire me to become

Except

A girl who's so empty of good things

She knows she won't

Ever be able to become

Anything.

WRITING EXERCISE: Life Events Journal

Hunter came over today. Dad just let him in the house without me even knowing it. I was in my room listening to his CD and singing at the top of my lungs when he showed up at my bedroom door. I finally have a real friend and then he sees me doing something embarrassing like singing into a hairbrush. Good thing Hunter thought it was funny.

Hunter had never been inside my house before. Thankfully Dad had finished a lot of work on the inside already. Even so, Hunter's house was a lot nicer than ours. But after all, he did have a real mom to make it a home. I not only had a dead mother, I had one who had left us.

Hunter and I talked about the plans for his go-cart for a while. He said his dad would probably never get around to rebuilding a car with him, so he wanted to make his go-cart look like a '57 Chevy.

Later I went to the kitchen to get us a snack. When I came back to my room, Hunter was reading the rough draft of my persuasive essay. I wished he'd at least picked up the final copy. I wasn't used to people reading my stuff. I wanted to grab it away from him, but before I could do anything, Hunter said, "This is really good, Ratchet! You should send it in for the newspaper's essay contest."

I was <u>supposed</u> to read the newspaper every day as part of my social studies work, but I hadn't picked up a newspaper in weeks. I didn't know anything about an essay contest.

"The winner gets their essay published in the paper. They also get fifty dollars," Hunter explained.

I told him I didn't know. "It's just an assignment I have to turn in. It's not really good enough to win anything."

"I think it is!" said Hunter. "Besides, how do you know if it's good enough unless you send it in?"

I told him I'd think about it, but I knew I'd never send it in. A persuasive essay about a park that was going to be history didn't seem like a winner to me, so what would be the point?

WRITING EXERCISE: Freewriting

Ever since I'd read the letter from Mom, the guilt about being mad at Dad weighed more than the car that was on top of the jack that slipped and crushed his thumb.

He didn't want to talk about the mystery box. And now I knew why. He didn't want me to know about Mom leaving. Better if I just think she's dead.

Maybe he didn't want me to feel bad about her not taking me with her.

Why didn't she? The letter said she didn't love Dad anymore, but I don't know what she thought about me. She didn't even mention my name.

The Mom I remember would never leave. Especially her daughter. But maybe that means I don't really remember her at all.

WRITING EXERCISE: Freewriting

It's hard for me to have a dad like Dad.

But it's harder for me to know that my mom was like Mom.

I wish I never knew.

WRITING EXERCISE: Life Events Journal

Hunter called me and told me to come over. Said he had something to show me. Something for his '57 Chevy. But when I got there he wasn't home. His mom told me he'd be right back. He had just gone to run some homework over to a friend's house. I hoped it wasn't Evan's.

Hunter's Mom poured me some iced tea and sat with me at the table while I waited for Hunter to come home. As usual she looked like the "after photo" on one of those makeover shows: Her hair in its neat ponytail. Faded light blue jeans. V-neck T-shirt with polka-dot hearts on it. I sat looking like the "before photo," wishing there was a way to will myself to look just like her.

She talked about how glad she was that Hunter and I had become friends. She thanked me for helping him study for the go-cart test. And then she told me I had the prettiest blue eyes she'd ever seen. That's when it happened. Maybe it was an allergic reaction to all the attention and compliments or something, but I started bawling my eyes out.

Every tear was a wish—

I wished I'd never gotten mad at Dad.

I wished the jack had never slipped.

I wished my mom hadn't left.

I wished she'd loved us more.

I wished I could've stopped her from going.

I wished she hadn't hurt Dad.

I wished I'd never opened the mystery box.

I wished Hunter's mom was <u>my</u> mom.

I couldn't stop the tears or the wishes.

"Honey, what's wrong? What is it?" Hunter's mom

hugged me while I cried, but that only made me wish

for one more thing—that it hadn't been so long since

someone had hugged me.

Hunter walked in. I needed to explain why I was crying. But

if Dad didn't want <u>me</u> to know what was in the mystery box,

I knew he wouldn't want anybody else to know either. So I did

what Dad would've done. I stretched the truth. I told them I

was crying about Moss Tree Park. It was the only thing I could

think of, and thankfully they believed me. Hunter told me not

to worry. He said if anyone could save the park it was my dad.

I wished I would've let Dad save me from knowing that my

mom must've never really loved me.

Summary of newspaper article "Park Lovers Lose—Moss Tree Park's Last Day"

The decision is final. Moss Tree Park will be leveled. No more trees. No more grass. Loads of dirt will get dumped into the pond. And the swings, monkey bars, and slides will be taken down. After that, they'll pour lots of concrete over the whole thing to make a parking lot for the strip mall. Then they'll start building. Lots of people would rather have a park than a mall, but the people who want the mall wear suits and are more important. So they win.

WRITING EXERCISE: Poetry

If I could change

Some things

I'd start with

Having a different mom.

But instead I'll

Like Dad more

And love him enough

So that he'll know

That Mom made a mistake

When she left.

If I could change

Some things

I'd be one of the

Important people,

And I'd make Dad

One too.

And we'd save the park

Together.

But instead I'll

Ask Hunter's mom

To teach me how to

Make cookies,

And I'll make a whole bunch

for Dad

So he'll smile

And maybe forget

for a few minutes

That we lost the park

And Mom.

WRITING EXERCISE: Choose one type of graphic organizer and use it to organize information about a familiar topic.

Writing Format—VENN DIAGRAM: Overlapping circles used to organize information to compare and contrast different subjects.

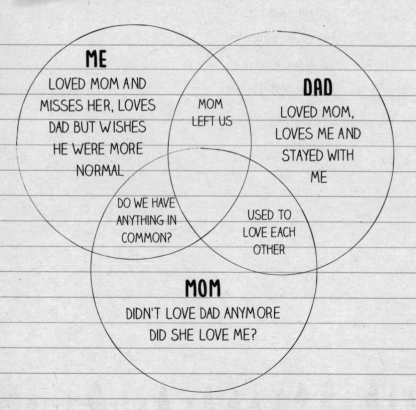

ME
LOVED MOM AND MISSES HER, LOVES DAD BUT WISHES HE WERE MORE NORMAL

MOM LEFT US

DAD
LOVED MOM, LOVES ME AND STAYED WITH ME

DO WE HAVE ANYTHING IN COMMON?

USED TO LOVE EACH OTHER

MOM
DIDN'T LOVE DAD ANYMORE
DID SHE LOVE ME?

Dad was down the street helping someone whose car wouldn't start. I was changing the spark plugs on an SUV when Hunter came over. He was bummed out about Moss Tree Park just like Dad and I were.

After I finished the SUV, Hunter and I sat on the garage step. Dad's oldies station played in the background. When "fun, fun, fun" by the Beach Boys came on, I got up and switched it off.

"Hey," Hunter said. "I like that song."

"Well, there's nothing fun about losing Moss Tree Park."

As we sat together in the quiet garage, I realized how close Hunter was sitting. I wondered if he realized it too, but before I had time to find out, Hunter stood up and walked over to Dad's workbench.

"Maybe there is some fun," he said as he picked up a

screwdriver and held it like a microphone. "And so we can't have fun now that Prindle took the town's park away," Hunter sang to the tune of "fun, fun, fun."

We spent the next hour coming up with goofy lyrics for some of our favorite oldies songs. Then we spent the <u>next</u> hour after that singing them at the top of our lungs.

Here's one of our favorites:

(To the tune of "fun, fun, fun" by the Beach Boys)
Well, we cleaned up the trash and hoped we could help save the park now.
Mr. Moss wanted trees not a mall and a gray parking lot now.
But Dad lost his fight, and the park and the trees will be gone now,
And so we can't have fun now that Prindle took the town's park away.
And so we can't have fun now that Prindle took the town's park away.
Well, we'll all take our cars and we'll cruise them all over the town now.
And we'll trail Eddie J. and Prindle wherever they go now.

We'll keep it all up till they wish we'd just all

go away now.

And so we'll have some fun now that Prindle

took the town's park away.

And so we'll have some fun now that Prindle

took the town's park away.

Our song wouldn't save the park, but having a friend like

Hunter sure felt like it was helping to save me.

The next day Dad left a piece of paper on the kitchen table.

For Sale
1964 Mustang
Yellow
Ready for Restoration

So I asked Dad why he was selling the Mustang. Ever since I could remember, he always said he had big plans for that car.

"Just time to get rid of it," he said, but I didn't believe him. I knew he'd never get rid of that car unless he had to.

That's why when I found the letter on the counter under the sugar bowl, I knew Dad had stretched the truth again.

Dear Mr. Vance,

Due to recent circumstances and the fact that you are unable to fulfill your hours of community service, the county has changed your sentence to a monetary fine of $5,000. You will be given thirty days to remit payment to the county clerk's office in the form of cash or check.

Sincerely,
Officer Jenkins,
Community Service

Now I understood why it was "just time" to get rid of the Mustang, and the heaviness that pressed down on me every day just got heavier. This was all my fault. Dad couldn't pick up garbage because of his hand, and his hand had been hurt because of me.

Dad already lost Mom.

He was losing the park.

And now because of me he was losing the Mustang.

Today I had a great idea. Hunter and I could go to the library and find out more about Herman Moss. If we could find a way to prove he never wanted Moss Tree Park developed, we could save the park.

Dad had already searched for this at the library, but maybe there was something he missed, and maybe Hunter and I could find it.

Then we'd be able to save the park for Dad, and my heaviness might get a little bit lighter.

If only there had been a way to save Mom.

There was a letter on the kitchen table. Dad must've left it there while I was in the shower. It was a stamped letter addressed to me, which meant it came in the mail. How could that be? Who would write me a letter? I turned it over and read the return address on the flap of the envelope. *The Blainesfield Beacon.* The newspaper? Why would I get a letter from the newspaper?

I opened it and read:

$\longrightarrow$

Dear Rachel Vance,

We are pleased to inform you that your essay, "Save Moss Tree Park," is in our top ten for the Fifth Annual Essay Contest. All of our entries were outstanding this year, so your place in the top ten is quite an accomplishment.

Our judges are working now to make their final decision, and the first-place essay will be published in the Community Corner section of *The Blainesfield Beacon* next week.

Thank you for entering and congratulations on being one of our finalists!

Sincerely,

Martin Pardell
Martin Pardell, Editor

Maggie Verla
Maggie Verla, Essay Judge

Owen Nelder
Owen Nelder, Essay Judge

Anita Welch Wilkerson
Anita Wilkerson, Essay Judge

WRITING EXERCISE: Freewriting

An essay about a crazy guy and his daughter defending a park that's going to be developed? Why would Hunter think it was a good idea to have this published in *The Blainesfield Beacon*? Just to make sure everyone sees Dad's latest failure? Dad was already enough of a joke in this town. And now my essay would make it worse. Did we really need this?

WRITING EXERCISE: Write a conversation poem.

Writing Format—CONVERSATION POEM: A poem based on a conversation between two people.

"Forget it,"

Is what I said when Hunter came over to go
to the library with me.

"How could you?!"

Is what I asked when I showed him the letter
from *The Blainesfield Beacon.*

"Good-bye,"

Is what I said after he finished trying to
explain why he had done it.

WRITING EXERCISE: Poetry

If having a friend means

Having someone butt into your life

And take your stuff

   And do something with it

      You never wanted them to do

         Without even telling you,

I guess it's a good thing

I've <u>never</u> had a friend.

WRITING EXERCISE: Poetry

Mom left

And didn't tell me.

Dad knew the truth

And didn't tell me.

Hunter did something

Behind my back

And didn't tell me.

The mayor and Eddie J. have probably done

something

Behind everyone's back

And didn't tell anyone.

Stretching the truth is one thing.

Twisting and tangling it up

Until it turns into something that

Hurts people

Can be called

Lying, deceiving, and dishonest.

But no matter what you call it,

It all feels the same.

Like a big, fat slap in the face.

"LIES"

WRITING EXERCISE: Life Events Journal

After the whole thing with Hunter, I rode my bike to the library by myself. I was afraid he might show up there even though I'd made it pretty clear he wasn't welcome, but he didn't.

I sat at one of the reference tables with all the stuff the librarian had found for me about Herman Moss. There was lots of stuff because Mr. Moss has been an important person in Blainesfield a long time ago. He had been born and raised here and had planned on staying, but one article I found told about how his college sweetheart Anita Welch broke his heart, so he'd left town to seek his fortune somewhere else. He never ended up getting married or having a family, so he spent all his money buying land and building parks. When he died, he donated all his land, and because he loved trees so much, he made the condition that all his land could never be developed for anything other than parks. Dad had told me this part. He had even been able to find all the paperwork in all the other counties where Mr. Moss had donated land, but because Dad couldn't find the paperwork documenting his wishes for Moss Tree Park, the mayor and the city council could decide what to do with the land.

I stared at all the books, pamphlets, and newspaper articles spread out all over the table. Why had I thought I'd be able to find anything when Dad hadn't been able to? Dad never left a stone unturned. If there was something to find, Dad would've found it.

Dad and Herman Moss were actually a lot alike—lovers of trees and unlucky in love.

I looked back at the article about Herman Moss's college sweetheart. I wondered why Anita Welch had decided not to marry Mr. Moss.

Anita Welch. That name sounded familiar, but I didn't know why.

I cleaned up the library table and thanked the librarian. I rode home on my bike wondering if the Good Lord wanted us to love each other, why didn't he make it easier to do, or at least make it hurt less when you _did_ love someone but they didn't love you back?

WRITING EXERCISE: Poetry

I need a new word

for "sad."

One that means

    Not

    Having

    The

    Energy

    To

    Write

    A

    Sentence.

One that means

All the things you thought you knew

Aren't true

And now you're empty inside.

One that means

Your most important person

Misunderstood

What you did.

And now you're left alone.

This morning

Dad needed a new word

for "angry"

When he found me in my room

With the letters from The Box.

"What do you think you're doing?!"

"Did I teach you to be a sneak?!"

"I hope you're happy now!"

And he grabbed the letters

Right out of my hands.

Did he really think I was happy now?

The tires squealed

Louder than the fan belt

When Dad and the Vegetable Rabbit left.

I stayed,

frozen with regret,

The smell of fried chicken

And Dad's angry words

Hanging in the air.

My memories

Ripped

Out of my heart,

Twisted

By a tornado of truth.

Myself,

All alone.

Dad came back.

Later.

He took The Box

Stuffed the letters

Back inside.

Locked it.

And then

Wrapped black electrical tape

Around and around the box

Until it looked like a zebra.

He didn't say a word

Until later when we were working

On a fuel filter in a ford—

Dad was working one-handed

And telling me what to do.

"It wasn't you,"

He said.

"It was me.

She left because of me,"

Is all he said.

And I understood.

Both of us

Needed a new word

for "hurt."

WRITING EXERCISE: Poetry

A QUESTION-ANSWER POEM

When we finish the fuel filter

We wash our hands

Side by side

In the laundry tubs

Like we do every day

Trying to wash away

All the grease and grime.

But the question I ask

Is tougher than

The toughest grease.

"How come she didn't take me with her?"

And the answer I get

Can NEVER be washed away

No matter how hard I scrub.

"Because I wouldn't let her."

WRITING EXERCISE: Write a proposal for an upcoming project.

REVISION

SUBJECT: Ratchet

PROJECT DESCRIPTION: Turn my old, recycled, freakish, friendless, homeschooled, motherless life into something new.

REVISED PROJECT GOALS:

1. ~~Make a friend.~~ Forgive the friend I have.

   o ~~Use magazine makeover tips to improve my look.~~
   o ~~Sign up for "Get Charmed" class at the rec center.~~
   o ~~Cross my fingers and hope to make a friend.~~

2. ~~Be more like Mom.~~ Be more like Dad.

   o ~~Ask Dad questions about Mom.~~

~~o Search for things that are Mom's to help me~~
~~remember her.~~
~~o Try to be like Mom.~~

OUTCOME: TO BE AN ORDINARY GIRL WHO FITS IN HOPEFULLY ONE WITH A FRIEND. THE NEW ME.

The note I found taped to our front door:

R. V.

I sent in your essay because it was good.
I was trying to do something nice.
Sorry you're mad.

H. D.

WRITING EXERCISE: Poetry

I don't know

If it was Hunter's apology

Or knowing the truth

About why Mom didn't take me with her,

But I was sitting in my room,

My insides

Feeling not quite so heavy,

Looking at Hunter's note

And the letter about my essay,

Thinking about Moss Tree Park,

When it all becomes clear—

Anita Welch was A. W.

And Herman Moss was H. M.,

And their initials were carved

Into the tree at Moss Tree Park

And more importantly,

A. W. is Anita Welch Wilkerson

Whose name is at the bottom

Of my essay letter.

A judge for the contest.

Which means she was still alive.

Which means she might have a clue.

The clue we need to prove Herman Moss's wishes

Are really deeper than the roots of the trees

At Moss Tree Park.

WRITING EXERCISE: Life Events Journal

I accepted Hunter's apology by asking him to go to Moss Tree Park to see the initials in the tree. And sure enough, they were there just as I'd remembered them.

As soon as I told Hunter the whole story about A. W. he agreed that Anita Welch Wilkerson might have the clue we'd been looking for.

So we headed back to Hunter's house to use his computer to see if we could find out where Anita lived.

WRITING EXERCISE: Use a sensory chart to record the details of a scene.

Writing Format—SENSORY CHART: Use the five senses to organize the sensory details of a scene.

Sight

* Hunter's sandy blond hair
* Hunter's cute smile
* Hunter's excited eyes

Sound

* Computer keyboard clicking
* Hunter's mom calling, "Do you kids want a snack?"
* Hunter yelling, "Sure, Mom!"
* Microwave beeping and then pop, pop, popping

Smell

* Buttered popcorn
* Lilac perfume when Hunter's mom brought us popcorn and lemonade

Touch

* Hunter's mom's hand on my shoulder, when she said, "Hi, Ratchet!"
* Cold, wet glass in one hand
* Greasy, salty popcorn in the other
* Hunter elbowing me when he found out that Anita Welch Wilkerson still lived nearby

Taste

* Cool, sweet lemonade
* Buttery, salty popcorn

But what looked, sounded, smelled, felt, and tasted the best?

Being friends with Hunter again.

Ms. Welch Wilkerson lived in a nursing home on the very edge of town, and we had to bike on the long gravel road out of town to get there. Halfway down the road, we saw a car off to the side of the road almost in the ditch. When we got closer to it, we realized it was Pretty Boy Eddie and his shiny, black town car. It looked like he had a flat tire.

We stopped next to where he knelt on his suit coat looking at the tire. It wasn't just flat; it was blown apart.

Hunter asked him what had happened.

Eddie J. looked startled to see us.

He wiped his forehead with the back of his hand and said, "Don't know. Tire popped. I slammed on the brakes, and next thing I know I'm sliding sideways into this ditch. Like to scared the heck out of me."

Hunter and I parked our bikes off the road.

I asked him if he had a spare.

Eddie J. said he'd just call a tow truck.

I told him calling a tow truck for a flat tire was like calling an ambulance for a paper cut.

Eddie J. laughed. "You're Lamar Vance's daughter, aren't you? I thought I recognized you."

I wasn't surprised he recognized me. Dad saw Eddie J. at least once a week at some meeting, and he had seen Dad and me together around town plenty of times.

I told him I'd change the tire if he had a spare.

"What?" Hunter asked, sounding surprised.

I don't know if he was more surprised I was going to change a tire or that I was going to help Eddie J.

One thing Dad had taught me: "Ratchet, always use the smarts the Good Lord gave you to help people in trouble no matter who they are."

I knew Dad would've changed a tire for Eddie J. even though the two of them didn't see eye to eye on just about anything. Dad would have used the time to lecture him about something while he was doing it, but he would've helped him for sure. I would change the tire and save the lecturing for Dad.

"Now where would that spare be? In the trunk?" Eddie J. asked.

I couldn't believe he didn't know where his spare was.

Eddie sat in the car and popped the trunk. I walked

around to the back of the car to see what I could find. I found something all right. The trunk was full of papers. Eddie J.'s briefcase must have busted open when he slammed on the brakes and everything inside it had been scattered all over. I wondered if any of the papers had to do with Moss Tree Park. This could blow the case for Moss Tree Park wide open.

"Do I have a spare?" Eddie J. called from the driver's seat.

I knew if there was a spare it was underneath all the papers. I thought about looking through a few of them while I uncovered the jack, but before I had the guts to do anything, Eddie J. was standing right next to me.

"What the heck happened here?!" he yelled as he scrambled to collect the papers, shove them into a pile, and stuff them back into the briefcase.

As he did, I pretended I hadn't noticed the papers. I knew Eddie J. must've been flustered for a reason. He was usually as cool as a cucumber.

I lifted the compartment where the spare was and grabbed the jack. I headed around the side of the car so that Eddie J. wouldn't be suspicious about what I'd seen. I jacked up the car and waited for Eddie J. to finish organizing his stuff in the trunk. When I went back to the trunk for the spare,

I noticed that Eddie J. was sweating worse than when we'd gotten there.

I wiggled the spare out of the trunk. Plunked it on the ground and rolled it to the side of the car. I used the tire iron to loosen the lug nuts on the blown tire and handed them to Hunter who wasn't doing anything but standing around with his hands in his pockets. Then I pulled off the tire and laid it on the ground. I slid the spare into place, twisted the lug nuts on loosely, and then tightened them up with the tire iron. After lowering the jack, I put it and the flat tire back in the trunk, which didn't have one single piece of paper left in it.

Eddie J. and Hunter both watched me like I was performing brain surgery. I was finished in less than ten minutes. Unlike Eddie J., I never broke a sweat.

Eddie J. thanked me and tried to give me some money, but I wouldn't take it. He drove off leaving a cloud of gravel. When the dust settled, there was a piece of paper lying in the grass. It must've dropped when Eddie J. shoved all his papers back into his briefcase. I picked it up knowing that it might be a piece of paper that wouldn't need to be recycled in order to save a tree.

WRITING EXERCISE: Freewriting

If the Good Lord had been waiting to give Dad and me a break, the piece of paper from Eddie's J.'s trunk would've been his perfect chance, but as Dad says, the Good Lord works in mysterious ways. Out of all the papers that could've fallen out of Eddie's J.'s trunk, the one that did was Dad's plan for better placement of the sprinklers that water the lawn at the library. Dad had sent it to the mayor last week.

So I shoved the piece of paper into my pocket, and Hunter and I kept going toward the nursing home.

I wondered what the Good Lord was waiting for.

WRITING EXERCISE: Write a modern day fairy tale in which you are one of the characters.

Writing Format—FAIRY TALE: A fanciful story of legendary deeds and magical characters.

Once upon a time there was a girl named Ratchet and a boy named Hunter who were trying to save an enchanted forest. They knew the Wise Ms. Wilkerson, whose voice had special powers because she had once been a teacher in the village, was the only one who could help them.

Having the reputation of being old and persnickety, the Wise Ms. Wilkerson lived in the town nursing home, and Ratchet and Hunter did not want to go there because they knew the place was filled with strange smells and scary sounds, but they had no choice. A visit to the nursing home was their only hope. They believed the Wise Ms. Wilkerson was the only person who might be able to stop the foolish Prince Prindle from letting the town villain, Pretty Boy Eddie, bulldoze down all the trees in the enchanted forest and turn it into a strip mall.

As Ratchet and Hunter walked down the hallway of the nursing home, trying to ignore the strange sounds and breathing through their noses to avoid the weird smells, Ratchet asked, "What are we going to say to the Wise Ms. Wilkerson?"

"We'll just ask her about Herman Moss," Hunter said.

Herman Moss was the wizard who had created the enchanted forest. He and the Wise Ms. Wilkerson had been childhood friends.

"But she doesn't even know us. Why would she talk to us?"

"Old people love to talk about themselves," Hunter said. "When my grandparents visit, they never stop talking. We'll get her to talk."

When they got to her room, the two children wished they hadn't come. The Wise Ms. Wilkerson was a tiny, pale, wrinkly person sitting all hunched over in bed reading a big thick hardcover book. It was hard to imagine that she even had any regular powers, let alone any magical ones.

"Excuse me," Hunter said as he tapped on the door.

"I beg your pardon," she said, "but who are you two?"

Hunter introduced himself and then asked if they could talk to her about something. Both children still stood in the doorway. It didn't yet feel like they were being invited in.

"What in heaven's name would you two children want to talk to <u>me</u> about?" the Wise Ms. Wilkerson asked.

It wasn't hard to see how she had gotten her reputation. She already sounded annoyed, and they hadn't even asked her anything yet.

Ratchet wondered if Hunter had been wrong. Maybe not ALL old people like to talk.

"The enchanted forest," Hunter said.

"The enchanted forest?" the Wise Ms. Wilkerson sounded more surprised now than angry. "What about the enchanted forest?"

The Wise Ms. Wilkerson tried to push herself up a little in bed, but as she did, she winced as if she were in pain.

The children wondered why she hadn't used her magical powers to make herself healthy.

"My dad's trying to save it," Ratchet said.

"Save it?" the Wise Ms. Wilkerson asked. "Save it from what?"

"It's going to be turned into a strip mall," Ratchet said.

"What?!" Ms. Wilkerson exclaimed.

The children wondered where the Wise Ms. Wilkerson had been. All the local news channels and newspapers had been talking about the forest every day for the last year. If she was so wise and magical, how did she not know about it?

"I bet it's that confounded Prince Prindle," the Wise Ms. Wilkerson said. "That boy has been a pain in my side since he was a young lad, and now that he's grown up, he's a pain in everyone's side."

The Wise Ms. Wilkerson had been a schoolteacher—legend said that's where she had earned her magic powers. Prince Prindle had been one of her students.

"You two get in here this instant and tell me what's going on," the Wise Ms. Wilkerson demanded.

Hunter had been right after all. Old people _do_ like to talk.

The children explained everything that had been happening with the forest, and the Wise Ms. Wilkerson explained that she hadn't left the nursing home in years because of her arthritis. She didn't know anything about the fate of the enchanted forest because she had given up watching the news and reading the newspaper years ago. She said it was much too depressing.

By the time the children finished explaining everything, Ms. Wilkerson's pale face was pink with frustration.

"Well, I know, for a darn certain fact, that Herman Moss would NEVER have allowed that foolhardy Prindle to destroy the forest. And he would have made darn sure that all the paperwork would be filed accordingly. Which means only one thing," the Wise Ms. Wilkerson said.

"What?" Ratchet and Hunter both said.

"That Prince Prindle really did turn into a criminal like I predicted he would. He never could stand up for himself, and people like Pretty Boy Eddie have been talking him into cheating, lying, and stealing since he was in elementary school. If it weren't for his royal blood, he'd be rotting in prison somewhere. But let me tell you, his royal 'get out of jail pass' has just expired."

The children looked at each other.

"I may be old, and I may not be able to get out of this bed, but I've still got a little bit of magic left, and this is the kind of thing that's worth using it for. I'll be doggoned if I'm going to let my dear friend Herman Moss's legacy be bulldozed down."

Ratchet and Hunter couldn't believe it! The Wise Ms. Wilkerson really did have magical powers! And it sounded like she was ready to use them to help!

"Herman was such a sweetheart," the Wise Ms. Wilkerson said, looking like she was thinking of fond memories.

"How come you and Mr. Moss never ended up together?" Hunter asked.

Ratchet pinched Hunter in the leg. She couldn't believe he had just asked that.

"Oh, it's a long complicated story, but mostly it was because I was a fool," the Wise Ms. Wilkerson said wistfully.

"What do you mean?"

"Well, I was young, and Herman's passion to use his wizardry on parks and trees didn't seem too romantic to me at the time. He was a simple man with simple dreams. Flannel shirts and jeans. So I married Owen Wilkerson, who was more polished and refined, using his wizardry in much flashier ways. He was a kind man, and I loved him. He was stable with a good job, and we had a wonderful life, but he was no match for the passion and wizardry of Herman. And I realized as I got older that Herman had all the things I really wanted in a man on the inside, and the inside is the part of the person we really love."

The children didn't know what to say or do next because the Wise Ms. Wilkerson sat quietly looking off in the distance. Her silence lasted so long they thought maybe she had forgotten they were there.

Hunter finally cleared his throat.

"Well, enough of all that," the Wise Ms. Wilkerson said. "I intend to put a stop to all these shenanigans. You mark my words. Prince Prindle and Pretty Boy Eddie will <u>not</u> get away with this. It's the least I can do in honor of Herman."

"What are you going to do?" Ratchet asked.

"We're going to get Prince Prindle over here so that I can have a talk with him," the Wise Ms. Wilkerson said.

"A talk?" Hunter said disappointedly.

That didn't sound like very much of a plan, but the Wise Ms. Wilkerson didn't mess around. She had Hunter dial the phone for her to call Prince Prindle at his castle. When the secretary wouldn't put the call through because she said the prince was busy, the Wise Ms. Wilkerson said, "Well, I suggest you get him unbusy because if he doesn't talk to me right now, there will be even more severe consequences for him than I already have in mind."

Ratchet had never been to school, so she didn't know if all teachers talked like this, but the authority in the Wise Ms. Wilkerson's voice made it impossible not to do exactly what she said. The secretary put the call through. It was magic.

"Benson Prindle, this is the Wise Ms. Wilkerson. I'm sure you remember me."

There was a pause.

"I want you to stop whatever you're doing and come down to the nursing home right now."

There was another pause.

"Listen, Benson, I don't think you are grasping the importance of this matter. I want you down here now and I will not take no for an answer."

And she hung up the phone.

While the children waited for Prince Prindle to show up, the Wise Ms. Wilkerson asked some questions about Hunter and Ratchet. While Ratchet was talking, the Wise Ms. Wilkerson realized that Ratchet's essay had been in *The Blainesfield Beacon*'s essay contest.

"You're one of our finalists!" the Wise Ms. Wilkerson exclaimed. "Your writing is outstanding! Very powerful!"

"I told you," Hunter said.

Ratchet felt her face get hot.

"You two children should be very proud of yourselves for working so hard to save the enchanted forest. It's very noble."

"Thanks," they said.

Just then there were footsteps coming down the hall, and they all looked to see Prince Prindle walking toward them.

"Children," the Wise Ms. Wilkerson said, "I'd like for you to wait in the hallway."

They both obeyed. The Wise Ms. Wilkerson's voice really did have special power over people. Ratchet and Hunter sat in the chairs outside the room. Prince Prindle closed the door. Ratchet and Hunter turned to each other and both put their ears to the door at the same time.

"Benson Prindle," the Wise Ms. Wilkerson said, "you should be more than ashamed of yourself. What in heaven's name ever made you think that you could do away with Herman Moss's enchanted forest. You know as well as I do that Herman never wanted that land developed, and I'd bet all my money on the fact that there is or was documentation to prove it."

The children expected the prince to argue and talk back, but the power in the Wise Ms. Wilkerson's voice made it impossible to argue.

"Now I don't know what you and Pretty Boy Eddie did with the paperwork, and I don't know what the two of you are getting out of it, but you can be darn sure there's a way to prove that you have done something terribly evil."

Still not a sound from Prince Prindle.

"If you choose to continue with this ludicrous plan to develop the forest into a strip mall, I will hire my son, who is an attorney over in Redville, to uncover your criminal ways. I suggest you make this entire project disappear. Because you mark my words, Benson, I will spend my very last dime, as well as every last drop of my magical powers, to make sure you are served with the justice you deserve. Are we clear?"

Prince Prindle finally spoke. "Yes, ma'am."

The door opened, and Prince Prindle walked straight down the hall and out the door.

Ratchet and Hunter high-fived each other. Then Ratchet went in and gave the Wise Ms. Wilkerson a kiss on the cheek, and her cheeks turned from frustrated pink to a bright and rosy red.

WRITING EXERCISE: Freewriting

The problem with fairy tales is that they're make-believe, and the problem with bullies is that they'll always be bullies.

The six o'clock news reported that Moss Tree Park's trees would be cut down Monday by the Chain Saw Cousins Lumber Company.

I guess in the real world, Ms. Wilkerson's words weren't as magical as we had thought.

WRITING EXERCISE: Life Events Journal

The next day Anita Welch Wilkerson called to say she was going to talk to Mayor Prindle again about the park. "It's just not right what he and Eddie J. are doing," she said. "We still have a couple days. There has to be <u>something</u> we can do to stop it." Ms. Wilkerson planned to talk to her son about it too. But I knew it didn't matter anymore. This was it. We were going to lose the park.

WRITING EXERCISE: Freewriting

Who would've thought I'd ever feel bad for the boys in Dad's class? But I do—and I feel even worse for Dad. The go-carts are built and ready to race, but it's too late—the race is officially canceled. Right after Ms. Wilkerson called, Cruella de Vil from the rec center stopped by to say that without the park, there would not be a race. Just one more reason to feel bad about losing the park.

WRITING EXERCISE: Life Events Journal

On Monday morning, I sat at the kitchen table looking at *The Blainesfield Beacon* searching for an article to summarize for one of my social studies assignments.

When I turned to page four, I immediately saw my name: Rachel Vance—Winner of *The Blainesfield Beacon* Essay Contest. And there was my essay printed for the whole town to read.

Why would my essay win and be printed in the paper the very day the trees were going to be cut down?

My heart sank. I didn't want this in the newspaper. I didn't want people reading about the poor daughter of the crazy guy who wanted the park saved but didn't find a way to save it—it made Dad and me look pathetic. I felt sick.

I shoved the newspaper into the trash can, which in our house was considered a cardinal sin. Dad would have a fit if he knew I threw a newspaper into the garbage can instead of the recycling bin, but I didn't want to take a chance on Dad seeing my essay. It would've been like pouring salt in his wound.

And then the phone rang.

"Did you see it?!" Hunter practically yelled into the phone.

"Yeah, I saw it! And that's why I didn't want you to send it in. I don't want everyone reading my essay. It makes Dad and me look like losers."

"You're not happy you won?"

"We didn't win, Hunter! The park is history, remember?"

"Maybe because of your essay they'll change their minds."

But I knew it was way too late for that because I could already hear the Chain Saw Cousins Lumber Company starting up their chain saws.

WRITING EXERCISE: Poetry

Buzzing,

Cracking,

Branches

Breaking.

Moss

Tree

Park

falling.

Dad's

Heart

Splitting

In two.

And

So

Is

Mine.

WRITING EXERCISE: Poetry

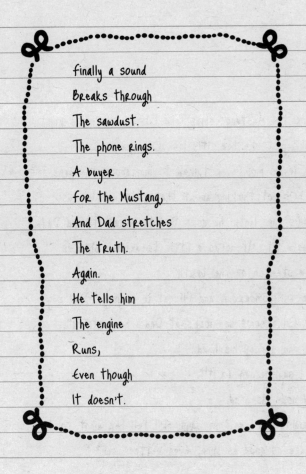

finally a sound
Breaks through
The sawdust.
The phone rings.
A buyer
for the Mustang,
And Dad stretches
The truth.
Again.
He tells him
The engine
Runs,
Even though
It doesn't.

WRITING EXERCISE: Choose two common sayings and write a situational incident which illustrates both.

The buyer for the Mustang comes, and I know who he is right away. He looks just like her. It's Ms. Wilkerson's son.

I wonder if his mom ever talked to him about the park. If she did, he's not thinking about that right now because he <u>loves</u> Dad's car. Until...he asks Dad to start it, and Dad says, stalling a bit, "It needs a little tweaking," which is more than a stretch of the truth.

"Give me till tomorrow, and I'll get it running," Dad says.

But Ms. Wilkerson's son looks at Dad's hand still all bandaged up and shakes his head.

"Wait!" I say. "I can do it!"

And Dad nods his head.

"She's right. She can," he says. "I'll tell her what to do. Her hands are as good as mine. Even better now."

And I feel some of the heaviness slip away as Dad's pride fills me up with something else. Something good.

(A SINGLE SPARK CAN BECOME A ROARING FLAME.)

"Maybe..." Ms. Wilkerson's son says. "But I don't know."

Dad does his magic, and before I know it, Ms. Wilkerson's son is giving Dad a down payment and driving away as the future owner of Dad's yellow Mustang.

And I wonder how I can be so happy and so sad at the same time.

(THERE ARE TWO SIDES TO EVERY COIN.)

WRITING EXERCISE: Freewriting

Dad takes the check and heads to the sheriff's office to pay his fine. As the Rabbit backfires out of the driveway, he tells me he'll be right back, and I wish so hard that he was driving the Mustang all tricked out and that he was using the money to buy back the park. But before Dad turns the corner, the fried chicken smell reminds me of reality and the sound of the chain saws in the background reminds me of just how much we're all

L
O
S
I
N
G.

WRITING EXERCISE: Poetry

While working on the Mustang,

Afternoon turns to evening.

The engine worse than Dad thought,

Dad promised it'd be done,

And though Dad may stretch the truth sometimes,

He doesn't break his promises.

Dad still can't use his hand

So he tells me what to do.

And I do the work,

But I'm tired.

My fingers sore from twisting nuts,

My palms blistered from squeezing pliers,

My neck stiff from straining to reach parts.

Covered in grease but too tired to scrub it all away,

I collapse into bed,

Leaving grease marks on my sheets.

The next day as soon as the sun's up

I hunch over the engine again,

And even though I'm more tired than I've ever been,

My heaviness turns into something else.

My anger about the mystery box and

My guilt about the accident

Slowly seep out of me like air

Leaking from a tire

With a very tiny hole in it.

And when the engine finally starts,

It runs like a charm,

And the old, stale air in my leaky tire is all gone.

And I feel myself being pumped back up,

Pumped back up with something,

And it feels like

It might be

The "something"

I've been searching for

All along.

WRITING EXERCISE: Write a cinquain.

Writing Format—CINQUAIN: A form of poetry with five lines. Each line contains a certain number of syllables.

"I'm proud"
Is what he says
But the way he hugs me
Says more than his words ever could.
My dad.

WRITING EXERCISE: Respond personally to a famous quote.

WHITNEY HOUSTON:

"She's (my mother) my teacher, my advisor, my greatest inspiration."

RATCHET:

He's (my father) my teacher, my advisor, my greatest inspiration.

What could a dad who loves me and won't ever

let me go

Teach me to think

Except that

I am worth everything in the world to him.

What could a dad who loves me and won't ever

let me go

Advise me to do

Except to

Dig deeper and try harder when things don't go

my way.

What could a dad who loves me and won't ever

let me go

Inspire me to become

Except a

Girl who's so full of good things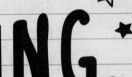

She knows she can do

 ANYTHING.

WRITING EXERCISE: Poetry

Sitting on the garage floor

Leaning against the workbench

My body so tired it's humming,

But all I hear is quiet..

Not just regular quiet,

But loud quiet.

Big quiet.

Quiet that fills up your ears

And echoes in your head

Making it ring like a bell.

The chain saws had stopped.

They had just started yesterday,

They couldn't be finished.

All the trees couldn't really be gone,

Not yet.

Not all of them.

So why would they stop?

WRITING EXERCISE: Freewriting

When Ms. Wilkerson's son, Adam, heard the Mustang's engine run for the first time, I think he was the happiest man in the world. He loved his new car, and he loved that he could drive it now thanks to Dad and me.

But when he drove off down the street to take it for a quick test drive, I could tell by the way Dad plunked himself down on the stool in the garage that he hated to lose that car, and then he told me why. It was supposed to have been my first car—he wanted to give it to me on my sixteenth birthday—those were his "big plans." And now he would never be able to do that.

But Dad didn't know that he'd already given me a much better gift than a car. While we worked on the Mustang together, it hadn't just been me being "Ratchet" making his job easier. It had been Dad relying on me to do the whole job, the job he couldn't do, and believing I could do it. And it was me seeing how much I already am like Dad and me realizing what a cool thing that really is.

I thought finding out about Mom would help me discover who I was really supposed to be, but now I knew that fixing up the Mustang with Dad had just showed me a whole lot more.

By the time Adam came around the block and stopped at the end of our driveway, I think he was <u>happier</u> than the happiest man in the world. And I think I was even happier than that.

Adam leaned his elbow out the window and said, "Can't thank you enough, Lamar. This car's a real gem."

"Pleasure doing business with you, Mr. Wilkerson," Dad said, standing up again.

"You two were probably a little busy this morning and didn't have time to see the newspaper, but check out page two," Adam said as he tossed a rolled-up newspaper up the driveway to us. Then he honked the horn and drove away.

I unrolled the newspaper, and Dad looked over my shoulder just as I turned to page two.

I couldn't believe it! There was my essay! They printed it again? I didn't want Dad to see this!

But then I saw right next to it that Ms. Wilkerson's son, Adam, had written an editorial about my essay. It wasn't just a little letter to the editor. He must've paid for a full-page spread because that's what it was. A collage of quotes about trees and a plea to the people of Blainesfield to save Moss Tree Park.

$\longrightarrow$

HELEN KELLER
To me lush carpet of pine needles or spongy grass is more welcome than the most luxurious Persian rug.

CANDY POLGAR
Alone with myself, the trees bend and caress me. The shade hugs my heart.

JOHN MUIR
When one tugs at a single thing in nature, he finds it attached to the rest of the world.

ALEXANDER SMITH
A man does not plant a tree for himself; he plants it for posterity.

WARREN BUFFET
Someone's sitting in the shade today because someone planted a tree a long time ago.

DR. SEUSS
I am the Lorax. I speak for the trees. I speak for the trees, for the trees have no tongues.

LUCY LARCOM
He who plants a tree, plants hope.

MARTIN LUTHER
God writes the gospel not in the Bible alone, but on trees and flowers and clouds and stars.

RACHEL VANCE
When you lose something you can never get back, you aren't ever the same person again.

Dear People of Blainesfield,

If you want to be part of saving something important, if you want to be part of doing something really big, if you want to be part of keeping Blainesfield beautiful, call Mayor Prindle's office and let him know you want Moss Tree Park saved.

Thank you, Rachel Vance, for reminding us what's really important.

Respectfully yours,
Adam Wilkerson

Before Dad or I could say anything, the phone in the garage rang.

WRITING EXERCISE: Life Events Journal

It was the editor of *The Blainesfield Beacon* calling for me. To tell me some really great news—MOSS TREE PARK IS SAVED!

After my essay appeared in the paper, the mayor got several phone calls from people about the park. Adam Wilkerson was one of those calls. He demanded that the destruction of the park be stopped, and even though the mayor told him "no way," he decided it was best to send away the Chain Saw Cousins Lumber Company until things settled down a little.

Adam knew that the mayor might be able to ignore a <u>few</u> phone calls about the park, but if enough people called he'd <u>have</u> to pay attention. So Adam decided to pay for a full page in today's *Beacon* so he could reprint my essay and add a few thoughts of his own. His idea worked because as soon as the paper came out this morning, the mayor's phone rang off the hook. The city council members had just met in an emergency meeting to reverse their decision about Moss Tree Park.

There would be a ceremony on Saturday at the park

where I'd receive an award for my winning essay, and Mayor Prindle would officially announce the restoration of Moss Tree Park.

But the best thing of all, better than even the park being saved, was when Dad heard the good news, he grabbed me and hugged me tighter than a race car hugs the inside lane during the last lap of the Indy 500.

I sure could get used to all this hugging.

WRITING EXERCISE: Life Events List Journal

Some Good News and Bad News

1. <u>Good</u>—Dad is the happiest I've seen him in a long time. He hasn't stopped whistling and singing in the garage since we got the good news. He just keeps saying, "Justice is like a train that is nearly always late."

2. <u>Good</u>—Since the park is saved, the go-cart contest is back on. I'm really happy for the boys, especially Hunter. And Dad too.

3. <u>Good and Bad</u>—The editor of *The Blainesfield Beacon* told me I have to accept my award at a formal ceremony. I have nothing to wear.

4. <u>Bad</u>—If I have to dress up for the ceremony, then that means Dad does too. He has nothing nice to wear either.

5. <u>Good</u>—I'm getting $50 for my essay, so I have plenty of money to go shopping for a new outfit.

6. <u>Bad</u>—I have no one to take me shopping to buy something to wear. Or more importantly, someone to tell me it looks good.

BUT the best "Good" thing of all is that now I know that fixing cars isn't the only thing I learned from Dad. With a little help from Hunter and Ms. Wilkerson's son, my words of persuasion changed people's minds about something really important. I was even more like Dad than I thought.

WRITING EXERCISE: Poetry

If having a friend means

Having someone butt into your life

And take your stuff

And do something with it

You never wanted them to do

Without   even telling you

Because they knew you wouldn't

And they knew it needed to be done

I guess it's a good thing

I finally have a friend.

WRITING EXERCISE: Poetry

If having a kind of crazy dad means

Having someone make your life

A little miserable

And make people stop and stare at you

When you don't want to be noticed

for all the wrong reasons

I guess it's a good thing

I have a kind of crazy dad

Because how else would I have learned

That sometimes saving something important

is the only way to save yourself

WRITING EXERCISE: Choose a strategy to organize ideas for writing an article.

Writing Format—5 W's CHART: An outline of your topic answering the following questions: who, what, when, where, and why.

WHO? Ratchet
WHAT? Saved the park
WHEN? In the nick of time
WHERE? Blainesfield
WHY? for Dad

WRITING EXERCISE: Write a psalm about yourself as if you are a hero.

Writing Format—PSALM: Poetry written in verses of two lines of any length. The first line makes a statement, and the second line repeats, opposes, or complements the first one.

Dad and I are the Three Musketeers minus one
HOPING TO BE VICTORIOUS.

I am the Robin Hood's helper of Blainesfield
TRYING DESPERATELY TO SAVE THE DAY.

Moss Tree Park is the spoils
WE LONG TO DIVIDE AND SHARE.

We're thanking the Good Lord
FOR CHOOSING TO BLESS US ALL NOW.

It took me three days to get up the guts to ask Hunter's
mom to take me shopping to buy a new outfit for the Moss
Tree Park ceremony, but I couldn't believe how happy she was.
She acted like I was doing her a favor. She said she always
wanted to have a daughter. I kind of wanted to say, "That's
funny, I always wanted to have a mom," but I didn't.

We went to the mall in Redville, the next town over. Hunter's
mom said she knew the perfect place. And she was right. She did.
We found lots of cool clothes, and I tried on more outfits in one
afternoon than I've tried on in my whole life.

At first I felt funny having Hunter's mom compliment me
on how I looked each time I came out of the dressing room.
I felt awkward standing in front of the three big mirrors
in clothes that made me look like someone else. But after a
while I forgot about acting shy. I got more excited with each

new thing I tried on. Maybe I'd be able to create my own style after all.

We were having so much fun.

Hunter's mom brought me different sizes and colors when things didn't fit or look right. She hung up all the clothes that I'd already tried on. It was like I was a rich famous person with a personal shopper who was also my best friend.

And then something awful happened.

The saleslady came in when I was standing in front of the mirror in a flowered sundress trying to decide which print I looked best in and she said to Hunter's mom, "Here's a necklace that goes nicely with that. Have your daughter try it on."

It's hard to remember what happened next because my head felt like I'd just gotten off a merry-go-round. My skin got cold and clammy, and the next thing I knew I was on the floor in a heap of tears and cotton floral print. It was as if a super magnet had pulled me to the floor, and I couldn't get up. I was scrunched up in a ball with my face in my hands sobbing so hard I almost couldn't breathe.

Hunter's mom crouched next to me and rubbed my back with one hand, while she dug some tissues out of her purse with the other. I knew this time I was going to have to tell her the truth.

I was crying about Mom.

"Let's go get something to drink in the food court," she said.

So we did. That's when I told her that I had a mom who didn't care about me. And even though I was crying again when I said those words, once I said them out loud I felt like a transmission that had just been flushed.

The words were true. I couldn't change them. I couldn't change that Mom had left. But I had to change the way I thought about the person who had been my mom.

I also had to change the way I thought about Dad. Yeah, he was weird—he didn't comb his hair or look like other normal dads and saving the planet for the Good Lord sounded kind of crazy to most people—but Dad was mine. He was my most important person. He loved me. He always stuck by me. And he always did what he thought was best for me. Even though most people thought he was crazy. I knew that deep down a lot of people thought he was smart. Most importantly I did.

Hunter's mom just listened as I talked. First about Mom. And then about Dad. I couldn't always look at her as I talked through my tears. But every time I looked up, she was looking right at me. And she kept her hands on top of mine as she listened.

When I finished talking and crying I felt like I'd just run a marathon. I was so exhausted. I could've put my head on the food court table and fallen asleep right there in the middle of all the burgers, fries, and ice cream.

Then Hunter's mom said the smartest, nicest thing. "Ratchet, you're a wonderful girl. And no matter how many wrong things you think your mom did, there's one thing she did that was an absolute miracle, and that was to have a daughter as beautiful and as smart as you."

WRITING EXERCISE: Freewriting

I told Dad.

I guess I shouldn't have.

But I did.

Because I had to.

Talking to other people is fine.

But Dad is my most important person.

I have to be able to tell him.

He has to be able to listen.

He listened all right. But then, he threw a wrench across the garage. Not at me. Not at anything really. But it was still scary.

Dad yells a lot at all kinds of people about all kinds of things. But I've never seen him hit anyone or throw ANYTHING. I didn't think me talking to Hunter's mom about Mom leaving would make him do that. I guess I was wrong.

WRITING EXERCISE: Life Events Journal

I wish I could be more excited about the ceremony to accept my award, but Dad's up on the roof, and I don't know if he's ever coming down.

After throwing the wrench, he took a box of shingles up there and he's been pounding ever since. Now my head is pounding too.

I'm going over to Hunter's in a while. His mom's going to help me fix my hair. I'm already wearing the outfit we bought. We went back and bought it after we talked at the food court the other day. But wearing the new outfit, having my hair look good for a change, and finally feeling like I look a little normal on the outside won't mean anything. Not if Dad doesn't show up. Because without him there, I won't feel normal on the inside.

The editor told me I should have a short acceptance speech ready, and I wrote one. But it's not for the audience. It's for Dad. So if he doesn't come...

WRITING EXERCISE: Poetry

Normal might be good

for some people

But I must not be one of them.

I go to the ceremony

With Hunter and his mom.

I look the most normal

I've looked in my whole life.

My clothes are just right.

My hair looks good.

So how come I feel out of place?

I fan myself with a program

While I turn around in my seat

Looking for Dad.

He's always easy to spot,

But I don't see him anywhere.

The microphone buzzes with feedback,

And Mayor Prindle heads for the stage.

I look at Hunter and his mom

Sitting on either side of me.

I'm with normal-looking people.

But I still don't feel like I fit in

Until I turn around in my seat

One last time

And see my dad

Standing way in the back

At the edge of the park.

I could tell

He had <u>tried</u> to comb his hair.

(But he still looked like Albert Einstein.)

He had <u>tried</u> to shave.

(But he must have used a very dull razor.)

He had <u>tried</u> to wear something nice.

(But his sports jacket was way out of style

And didn't fit at all.)

But it's the T-shirt he has on

Under the sports jacket that makes me smile

And makes me feel like I fit in right where I'm

supposed to.

The T-shirt says, "Everybody needs a Ratchet."

I had given it to him for Christmas

When I was eight.

I didn't even know he still had it.

Dad did <u>not</u> look normal,

But he was there.

And he had come for me.

<u>He</u> was my normal,

So I give the speech

I wrote for him.

Thank you for choosing my essay.

And thank you for saving Moss Tree Park.

Today our little Blainesfield world has changed,

And we should all be proud.

I learned about changing the world from a very important person.

He's not important the way most people are important—

He doesn't drive a fancy car.

He doesn't make a lot of money.

He doesn't have a big important job.

But he's MY most <u>important</u> person

Because he's taught me about what's <u>important</u>.

He's taught me how things work.

He's taught me to work hard.

He's taught me that the Good Lord values the Earth.

And because he does, we should too.

He's showed me how to love

By always being there for me.

And he made sure I felt loved.

To show him how well I learned his lessons,

I dedicate my award and Moss Tree Park

To my dad.

WRITING EXERCISE: Respond personally to a famous quote.

LOUISA MAY ALCOTT:

"What do girls do who haven't any mothers to help them through their troubles?"

RATCHET:

The Good Lord gives them a dad who loves them like my dad loves me.

WRITING EXERCISE: Life Events Journal

A week later at the Moss Tree Park Go-Cart Races, Dad was the guest of honor.

Not only because he had been the first one to really care about saving the park, but also because he was the reason all the boys in his class had the coolest go-carts the race had ever seen.

They were all made out of recycled materials: two-liter soda bottles, old crates, hubcaps, bicycle seats. You name it, you could find it somewhere on some car. Jason had made his entire car out of wood from an old dresser. He actually sat in a drawer to drive the thing.

It made me proud to have a recycle-crazy guy for a dad.

The cover girls were there admiring the boys' go-carts and trying to get the boys to admire them. I was thankful Hunter wasn't paying attention to any of the girls, and I was glad I had ended up creating my own style instead of "getting charmed." I felt comfortable and thought I looked sort of cute in the capris and fitted T-shirt Hunter's mom had helped me pick out when we went back to the mall for a second shopping trip. I guess I wasn't completely like Dad. I still cared about what people thought of me. Especially Hunter.

That day at Moss Tree Park was one of the best days of my life for lots of reasons.

One of the funniest things was Evan's go-cart. His brother wanted to make sure Evan's car was better than anyone else's because he was even more of a show-off than Evan, but his plan backfired in more ways than one.

His car looked ridiculous next to all the recycled cars because it was all shiny and new. It looked like a toy model that a little kid put together. The other cars were creative and had personality.

But the way Evan's car looked was only part of the problem. Evan's go-cart literally <u>did</u> backfire at the starting line because just after the beginning of the race, he blew a gasket. The car didn't get more than ten feet down the track. The recycled cars left him in the dust. It was great!

Even though Dad was the guest of honor, most of the people there watching the race still thought he was a little nuts. He was dressed in a T-shirt the boys had given him that said "Genius at Work" on the front and "Real Men Recycle" on the back. Dad cheered his head off as the boys' go-carts circled the track. Every time one of the boys finished, he jumped up and down like a five-year-old at the circus, and after all the boys crossed the finish line, they surrounded Dad, slapping him on the back and saying things like, "You're the best, Mr. Vance!" and "We couldn't have done it without you!" Hunter had been right. I <u>was</u> lucky to have a dad like Dad. The Good Lord had given me a break after all.

Before Dad even stopped jumping up and down, Hunter and the other boys came over and handed me a big, flat box.

"What's this?" I asked.

"Just open it," Jason said.

So I did. Inside was a long, skinny sugar cookie with squiggles of frosting all over it. It looked like a sword or a dagger or something, but I knew what it was supposed to look like—a ratchet.

"My mom helped us make it," Hunter said.

"And we all signed it," Jason added.

"We just wanted to say thanks," Hunter said.

I didn't care what the cookie looked like. I didn't care what it tasted like. I didn't care that I couldn't read one single name written on it. None of that mattered when you finally have real friends.

My life really wasn't all that different than it had always

been, but somehow it sure felt like something had changed. It felt like my new style wasn't just about the way I looked on the outside. It had more to do with how I felt on the inside. Finding out the truth about Mom wasn't easy, and it sure didn't make me feel more normal, but I would never have known how much Dad loved me if I hadn't found out Mom left.

After the race, we planted trees to replace the ones that had been cut down, and we celebrated as if it were Herman Moss's birthday with a great big cake. The best part was that thanks to Ms. Wilkerson, the trees we planted had been donated by Eddie J. She had shamed him into donating them by telling him it was the least he could do after being such a big bully.

Then we all ate burgers compliments of the owners at Mama Mack's, who had set up a booth in the park. Marty from Gas Gulp had frozen candy bars available, not for free, but for a very cheap price, of course. Hunter's dad was even there, and Hunter had more fun showing his dad how the engine in his '57 Chevy go-cart worked than he did driving his go-cart in the race. His dad seemed really impressed with everything Hunter knew about his engine, and I had a feeling the two of them might just get around to rebuilding a car after all.

Ms. Wilkerson and I sat in the shade at a picnic table and

ate lunch. Her son Adam had hired a van from her nursing home to bring her out to the park. He thought she should be there since she was the one who put her teacher's voice to work one last time to try and help save the park, and even though it took a little more than a stern teacher's voice to do it, she deserved some credit.

While Ms. Wilkerson and I finished our burgers and sat licking our melting candy bars, I watched Dad, who was too busy to eat. He was following the mayor around and telling him about a new solar-powered air-conditioning system. He wanted the mayor to put it in all the town's public buildings.

Ms. Wilkerson saw me watching Dad and said, "You know, your daddy reminds me so much of Herman Moss, and you remind me a little bit of myself. Don't be like me and let the world fool you into thinking your daddy's not a good man. He may never be the mayor or have the kind of job you think makes him <u>look</u> good, but I can tell you, his heart's in the right place, and that's what really matters."

The thing is, I didn't need Ms. Wilkerson to tell me that. My heart already knew it.

Turns out I didn't really need a new life—I already had a pretty good one—not a perfect one—but one that I could feel all right about.

WRITING EXERCISE: Poetry

If only seeing your own life

The way you should

Were easy,

But it's not.

I wouldn't have spent

So much time

Wishing

Things were different.

I wouldn't have spent

So much time

Worrying

About not being normal.

I wouldn't have spent

So much time

Writing

About wanting something new.

I wanted the

White pages

And the cool, cardboard cover
To somehow change
"Something,"
But the only thing
That really needed to change
Was
The way
I thought
About
Me
And
My
Weird,
Wonderful
Life
With
Dad.

ACKNOWLEDGMENTS

Authors are not supposed to use cliches, but I'm going to use one anyway: this book is my dream come true. My dream to publish a children's book began many years ago, and it would never have happened without some very important people.

To Esther Hershenhorn and Sharon Darrow, my very first writing teachers and friends who welcomed me into SCBWI and always willingly shared their knowledge and expertise, as well as their friendship.

To Patty Toht, Greg Daigle, Ruth VanderZee, Ellen Carroll, Darcy Zoells, and Michelle Schaub, my first critique group—wonderful writers and fantastic friends.

To Karen Palumbo, Sue LaNeve, Greg Neri, Mickey Davis, Madeleine Kuderick, Molli Nickell, and Karleen Tauszik, who were the first to see Ratchet and believe in her. Thank you for helping me figure out how to write this book and for becoming my new writing family in Florida.

To Holly Root, my agent, thank you for believing in me and my writing and not giving up when the going got long.

To Aubrey Poole, my editor, who always shared my excitement for Ratchet. Thank you for loving my book and working so hard with me to make it better.

To all the people at Sourcebooks, thank you for paying attention to every detail so that my book became something even better than what I had ever imagined it could be.

To Martha Alderson, whom I've never met, but whose books and DVDs about plot were invaluable. Thank you for all you taught me!

To my family and friends who supported me along the way and gave their encouragement even when they may have thought I was crazy to have kept trying for so long—thank you!

This book would not have happened without Ron and Chaylee, who cheered me on all the way. Thank you for being so proud!

Lastly, and most importantly, I thank the Good Lord for His unending grace and faithful blessings along the way.

ABOUT THE AUTHOR

Photo credit: Janet Nelson

Nancy J. Cavanaugh lives in Florida with her husband and her daughter. She spends her summers eating pizza in her former hometown of Chicago. *This Journal Belongs to Ratchet* is her first book, but she has been writing for almost twenty years.

Like her main character, Nancy is pretty handy with a ratchet and is able to take apart a small engine and put it back together. In addition to her mechanic's hat, Nancy has been an elementary and middle school teacher, as well as a school library media specialist. One of her favorite parts of writing for children is being able to say "I'm working" when reading middle grade novels. She hasn't read an adult book in years.

Visit her at www.nancyjcavanaugh.com.